THE
TIME TRAP

PETER CORRIS

THE TIME TRAP

Incorporating characters created
by Bill Garner and Peter Corris
for the ABC TV drama *Pokerface*.
This book is based on a story outline by Bill Garner.

HarperCollinsPublishers

HarperCollins Publishers

25 Ryde Road, Pymble, Sydney NSW 2073, Australia
31 View Road, Glenfield, Auckland 10, New Zealand

First published in Australia in 1994

National Library of Australia
Cataloguing-in-Publication data:

  Corris, Peter, 1942-
  The time trap.
  ISBN 0 7322 5016 1
  I. Garner, Bill. II. Title.

A823.3

Cover illustration by Mark Roxburgh
Cover design by Robyn Latimer
Typeset by Midland Typesetters, Maryborough, Vic.
Printed by McPherson's Printing Group, Victoria

9 8 7 6 5 4 3 2 1
97 96 95 94

for Phillip Knightley

~ 1 ~

Crawley's intercom buzzed and he fumbled for the right switch to hit. 'Yes?'

'Mr Crawley, there's a gentleman downstairs who demands to see you. He has no appointment. He says his name is Luck.'

Everything about the secretary's voice and manner irritated Crawley, but she came with the job. Incredibly, to himself and most other members of the Federal Security Agency, he had been elevated to the post of Acting Director. The incumbent was attending a security conference in London; the assistant director was ill and Crawley was 'it'. 'Luck? The only Luck I've ever heard of is on TV. Would you say he's bad luck or good luck?'

The secretary was without humour. 'Correction, sir. The name is Huck.'

'Send him in, Carol.'

Crawley got up and walked across the pale grey carpet. He was in his socks, not out of respect for Hector Bain's carpet, but because the shoes he had bought the day before pinched. It irritated Carol Mainwaring that Crawley opened the door to his callers instead of staying behind his desk. To see him standing in the doorway in his socks might send her home with a migraine. Crawley wore drill trousers and a blue cotton shirt. The knot of his dark brown tie was slipped down several centimetres inside the open neck of the shirt and his linen jacket was hung over the back of his chair, gathering more creases.

A door opened and Huck came lumbering towards him, pulling off his cap, showing his tanned, bald head.

1

Carol Mainwaring teetered along behind in her high heels and slim-fitting skirt. 'You have an appointment at ten, Mr Crawley.'

Crawley gripped Huck's hand. 'Gidday, Hucky. He might have to wait a bit, Carol.'

'It's Sir Ian Brewer of United Transport.'

'Then he'll have plenty to think about while he's waiting. He's going broke. Come on in, mate.'

Crawley stood a little over 180 centimetres and was powerfully built but Graeme Huck made him look small. Huck's large frame was well covered but he was not obese as he had been back when he'd been an FSA field officer. Retired to the south coast, he spent his time fishing, mending boats, rabbit hunting and walking. He drank more tea than beer. He stared at the pastel decor of the office, the glass-topped table, the leather reclining chairs.

'Christ,' Huck said. 'I never thought I'd see you in a joint like this, Creepy. What's going on?'

Crawley sat in an armchair and gestured for Huck to do the same. 'The top boys are junketing or away sick. They put me in for a bit because they reckoned I wouldn't want to stay. They were right. It's driving me nuts. What brings you to Canberra? You hate the place.'

Huck sat and reached into the breast pocket of his sports jacket. He removed a crumpled envelope. From another pocket he took a pipe and a tin of Erinmore flake tobacco. 'Can I smoke in here?'

'Go for your life.' Crawley reached for the envelope, opened it and extracted a newspaper clipping. It was taken from a south coast paper and headed, 'Local Librarian Drowns'.

Mr Barry May, 54, a retired public servant, was drowned yesterday after being swept from rocks north of Coota Coota where he was fishing. Mr May, who moved to the south coast several years ago, was popular as the volunteer driver of the 'Bookmobile' which brings books from the Nowra library to the towns of the area. He was also engaged in writing a history of the shire.

Mr May, a widower, is survived by his daughter, Ruth, who lives in Canberra.

'Friend of yours?' Crawley asked.

'Sort of. A good little bloke. You don't recollect him?'

Crawley looked at the cutting again and shook his head. 'Should I?'

'Not really,' Huck said. 'Quiet type. He worked as an FSA archivist in Melbourne from the year dot. Came up here for a bit but took early retirement. He remembered me when I went to the bookmobile to get some stuff on fishing. Sensible about it, he was. Just gently put a question or two and . . . you know.'

Crawley understood. Ex-members of the intelligence services didn't go about advertising their former occupation or carelessly accosting erstwhile colleagues, some of whom preferred to sever all old connections permanently. On the other hand, there was no one else they *could* talk to about their former lives and sometimes retirees became firm friends.

Huck's pipe was well alight and Crawley enjoyed the thought of Hector Bain's reaction when his sensitive nose picked up lingering odours in the Peruvian wall tapestry or a slight patina on the ceramic vases. Crawley had had the daily flower delivery cancelled, claiming allergy problems.

'We got on pretty well,' Huck said. 'He was knowledgable about the local area and I picked up a useful point or two.'

Crawley nodded. He was accustomed to Huck's circumlocutory style and aware of the various activities he engaged in on the coast—minor smuggling exercises involving fish, goods and personnel.

'It's all wrong, Creepy. Barry hated fishing. Had no patience for it. I took him out once and he was bored stiff. There was no way he'd be fishing off those rocks. No chance.'

Such vehemence was rare from Huck. A former MP in Korea and Victorian police Special Branch officer, he was steeped in cynicism and scepticism. Twenty years in the FSA had caused him to doubt everything and believe nothing. Crawley, equally incredulous, accepted Huck's statement. 'So he was killed?'

'Right. Now if you or me turn up floating face down in the fucking water some day, that's one thing. We've hurt people. But Barry May was quiet and gentle. He couldn't have had an enemy in the world.'

'You're tying yourself in knots, Hucky. If you're right he *must* have had an enemy. What about this local history thing? Maybe he uncovered some scam or found out that the town clerk's grandma was an Abo. Something like that?'

Huck shook his head. 'He'd have told me about it. That was just a hobby. Barry was a bit of a botanist. His research was more about the fucking trees and flowers than the people. His death has something to do with the FSA.'

Crawley shrugged. 'An archivist? Come on, Hucky.'

Huck held up two meaty fingers. 'One, there's all this stuff going on about protecting the files for fifty years, not thirty. That makes archivists a bit more important than usual.'

'That horse won't run,' Crawley said. 'It'll stick at thirty. People are too curious to wait. The journos are screaming already.'

'Maybe,' Huck said. 'Point two is that Barry told me a woman he used to work with, another archivist, turned up dead a couple of weeks ago. She was called Laura Hopkins, single, about fifty-five and in perfect health.'

'What happened to her?'

Huck was having difficulty with his pipe. There was no ashtray and he was using the saucer under a pot plant on the coffee table to deposit matches and scrapings. Some of the detritus spilled out onto the polished wood. Huck was an untidy man but a dogged one, and Crawley knew he would stay until he said what he'd come to say and got some satisfaction. 'She's supposed to have rowed herself out into the estuary at Launceston, tied the boat anchor around herself and jumped overboard. Barry said it was all bullshit, and that was strong language for him, poor little bugger.'

'So we've got two dead, retired archivists and you reckon something's up?'

'I *know* something's up, and who's to say it's going to stop at archivists? The way you could see it is two dead, retired FSA members living near the water . . .'

'I'm glad there's some self-interest here. I was beginning to think you'd gone soft.'

'This is just two we know about, Creepy. What if there's more? I read the papers, talk to a few people, keep in touch. There's some weird things going on in the intelligence game just now. I mean, think of that

Stuyvesant woman, selling the stuff.'[1]

'That was dealt with. You were there.'

'Look, I got to know Barry pretty well. We didn't see eye to eye on a few things, but we got along okay. He was against the fifty-year idea. I reckon it'd be a good thing myself. He was also all in favour of us . . . I mean the FSA, I mean *you*, now that you've gone so fucking high, responding more fully to Freedom of Information requests. You know how I feel about that.'

'Yeah,' Crawley said. 'You're a strong believer in the thick black felt pen approach.'

'Shit. Aren't you?'

'I don't know, Hucky. I'm just not sure of anything any more. That's another reason they jumped me in here. They reckon I'm just waiting out my time.'

Huck's excavated pipe was drawing again. He puffed thick blue smoke. 'Are you?'

'Maybe. Mandy thinks so. She's waiting for me to announce a lifelong ambition to go bee-keeping in the Monaro.'

Huck said nothing. His relationship with Crawley's wife Mandy had been uneasy from the start. Back when Huck was Crawley's superior and drinking companion, teaching him the ropes, and Mandy was a dutiful Melbourne housewife, they had been mutually contemptuous. Later, after Crawley leapfrogged Huck and had room to manoeuvre and Mandy pursued the radical academic path that eventually led her to a PhD, they had become semi-respectful enemies. When Huck took retirement rather than move from Melbourne to Canberra Mandy had welcomed the estrangement. But

---

[1] See *The Azanian Action* (1991)

Huck continued to surface in Crawley's personal and professional life, drawing him back into the old, aggressive, conservative, patriotic patterns which Mandy saw as postures.

'You know how it is, Creepy,' Huck said. 'You never really get out of it, no matter how far you go. Launceston's a long way from Canberra, but I reckon that poor Hopkins woman was still within arm's reach. It's a lifetime thing, mate. You could take your super and go and open a fucking mushroom farm out of Braidwood and there'd still be noises in the night.'

A long and intensely philosophical delivery for Huck. Crawley was inclined to acknowledge the truth of it, although he knew that the lifelong entrapment of intelligence agents was a two-way street—the system had clinging tendrils, but its roots were vulnerable if former agents decided to expose them. He remembered talking with a friend, an executive in advertising, about Elvis after they had listened, drunkenly, to a CD of 'The Sun Sessions'.

'Greatest stuff he ever did,' Crawley had said. 'All in that first year or two when he was a real rocker. Downhill to crooning, crap movies and Las Vegas after that, poor bastard. He got screwed.'

'He spread 'em,' his friend said. 'But Jagger and the smart boys learned from that. Did you hear how the Stones broke a bum record contract? Put down a track called 'Star Fucker'. Dared the company to release it. Company backed off. You can screw the screwers, root the rooters, if you know how. 'Course a public service wanker like you doesn't have to worry about things like that. Right, Ray?'

Crawley smiled at the memory. 'What do you want me to do, Hucky?'

'How busy are you?'

Crawley glanced across at the light scattering of paper on the desk. These days computer-delivered electronic mail and faxes had replaced the endless file folders. Crawley seldom switched the computer on and spent more time dealing with bureaucratic snags via the telephone than handling intelligence data. 'Not busy,' he said.

'You could check on the two dead 'uns and see if they've got any mates in recent times.'

Crawley crossed to the desk and picked up a pencil. 'Give me the names again.'

'Barry May and Laura Hopkin or Hopkins, I'm not sure which.'

Crawley scribbled. 'Okay. You know there's a big cull of the records on? A lot of stuff getting chucked out.'

'Shit. Why?'

'Apparently in the transfer of the files to CD Roms they've found a lot of stuff not worth preserving.'

'Who decides?'

'Hector and others like him.'

'Terrific.' Huck heaved himself from the chair. Ash and tobacco flakes fell on the carpet. 'This show has gone to the dogs. I don't know why you stick it.'

'So I can do favours for old mates like you. What are you going to be doing? Want to stay at our place?'

Huck shook his head. 'Your missus'd poison my food.'

'She's mellowed. She took a job in the environment minister's office. Now she's got some idea of how hard it is to get a bent paperclip straightened.'

'Thanks, anyway, Creepy. I'm getting a plane in an hour. I just wanted to see you. I'll sniff around back on the coast.'

The two men moved towards the door. Crawley was acutely aware of the incongruity of it all—shoeless, ushering his former workmate from the director's office. 'Just out of interest, Hucky. What exactly was Barry May's reaction to your views on the fifty-year rule and FOI?'

'He laughed like a drain,' Huck said.

~ 2 ~

Crawley's meeting with Sir Ian Brewer was brief. The transport magnate, after years of prosperity, was presiding over a failing empire. He had become convinced that he was a victim of industrial espionage and sabotage, that his competitors had planted enemies in his midst. Could the FSA identify and eradicate these vermin? The Agency had recently taken on consultative roles of this kind as money-making enterprises. The practice was despised by Crawley but enthusiastically pursued by Hector Bain.

'Identify perhaps,' Crawley said, 'but removal would be your problem. A matter for the police.'

Brewer, an overweight, florid figure in his sixties, looked disgusted. 'I was hoping for a bit more action than that.'

'If you were thinking of freeway foundations or high-temperature incinerators, forget it. I can give you some de-buggers, systems analysts and the like. That's about all.'

'When does Hector Bain get back?'

'In about ten days.'

'I'll take it up with him.'

Crawley, still in his socks, stood up behind the desk. 'You do that, Sir Ian. I'll put the import of this meeting on the record, of course.'

Brewer scowled and stalked out of the office.

Crawley worked in a desultory way on the routine matters at hand—doubts about the identity of a Cambodian refugee, several refused and re-submitted requests for telephone taps and mail interceptions, a report on the financial interest held by a federal MP in a pornographic video production outfit. His mind kept returning to Huck's questions. Eventually he shoved the memos and other documents aside and scrabbled under the desk for his shoes. He walked out of the office, past Carol Mainwaring, who was tapping at her keyboard while cradling a phone under her chin. Crawley could never understand how she could be so busy and her boss so under-occupied.

'Mr Crawley.' There was alarm in the secretary's voice.

'Yes, Carol?'

'Would you mind telling me where you are going?'

Crawley smiled when he saw that she was craning forward to see whether he was wearing shoes or not. He lifted his foot to show her one of the offending slip-ons. 'I'd rather not say. Who are you talking to?'

'Well, I . . .'

Crawley put his index finger to his lips. 'Need to know. I quite understand.' He walked quickly from the office.

It had taken him weeks to learn the geography of the FSA building in Canberra, and he could still make mistakes—open a door he thought led to a corridor to find a furtive smoker in a storage room, go down stairs to avoid the slow elevators to meet an unaccountably locked fire door. He did, however, know where to find Boris Stein, the computer expert who'd worked in Melbourne with Huck and Crawley and who had transferred happily to Canberra to a world of more megabytes, terminals and networkings. Boris had been moved sideways from operations to research and development and seemed not to notice the difference. Crawley marched into his office without knocking because to knock made no difference—Boris would be staring at a screen, and he would look up when it suited him and not before.

The small room was an electronic junkyard with terminals, keyboards, disks, monitors, printers and multi-point power plugs covering every surface. Computer manuals and magazines spilled from shelves and the waste paper bins overflowed with reject printout sheets. Boris was tapping frantically at a keyboard as lines of coloured print and figures scrolled down the screen in front of him. Crawley browsed through a magazine, not understanding one word in a hundred, while he waited. Eventually Boris said 'Shit', touched a key that blanked his screen and pushed his chair away from the terminal. He was small, egg-headed, and all his energy seemed to be packed into the space behind and above his eyes and translated to his fingers. His physical movements otherwise were slow and awkward.

'Crawley. What a pleasure! But you shouldn't have come down here. Why didn't you send for me? I'd have come sprinting up to the director's office—never been in there. Has he got a terminal?'

'Drop in any time you like, Boris. Of course he has. It's pale grey like all the rest of the decor. Don't ask me anything else about it, I couldn't tell you.'

'You're a neanderthal. Well, I've just wasted the morning so far. What can I do for you?'

Crawley asked him to access the files of Laura Hopkin or Hopkins and Barry May. 'You know all the short cuts, Boris. I don't want to buggerise around going through channels. I strongly suspect all Hector's mates have been worded up to block everything I do.'

'All power is illusory. There's probably someone blocking Hector.'

'Deep,' Crawley said. 'Send up the printouts in a security envelope, my eyes only.'

Boris sighed. 'I don't have to send them. I can transmit the data to you and you can print them out yourself, or your secretary can. What's her name?'

Crawley told him. Boris turned on his machine and tapped keys. 'Got her. Can you tell me what these people did? Might speed things up.'

'They were archivists.'

'All right. Jesus, I just had an idea!'

'About what?'

'You wouldn't understand. What I was working on. Anything else, Crawley? I want to try this idea out.'

'Is there any way you could scan the records for recently dead FSA members?'

'How recently?'

Crawley shrugged. 'This year. Say, six months.'

'Easy.' Boris was flexing his fingers. His pale grey eyes behind his spectacles seemed to be making intimate contact with the glowing screen.

Crawley replaced the magazine. 'Thanks, Boris. This has priority over your brilliant idea, remember. S.a.p.'

'Right. How's Huck?'

Crawley stared. 'Huck's fine. Why d'you ask?'

Boris smiled, took off his glasses and polished them with a tissue. 'Everything is logged, Crawley. I happened to see a quick check being run on Graeme Leslie Huck when I was looking for something else. I can't imagine him coming here and not seeing you.'

'Jesus.'

'I can offer your inquiries a certain degree of protection,' Boris said with a self-satisfied smirk. 'You've come to the right person, Mr Acting Director. Is that what you want?'

Crawley thought about Carol Mainwaring and the likelihood that he'd have to ask her how to operate the computer and printer. 'No, Boris. Don't bother. I mean, there's no need to broadcast it far and wide, but don't go to any trouble.'

Boris nodded, gazed at the screen, seized his mouse, and Crawley knew he was dismissed. He wandered through the passages, past the noticeboards carrying announcements for golf tournaments and social functions. Crawley's major sport was squash, at which he was a fierce competitor, but he was aware lately of a fall-off in the number of partners as his colleagues aged and switched, he suspected, to golf. He stopped at the canteen and bought a suspiciously soft plastic-wrapped salad roll and an apple. Reluctantly he made his way back, past the critical eye of Carol Mainwaring, to the director's office. Once inside he kicked the shoes off and crossed to the bar fridge discreetly concealed by a teak laminate. The room smelled of air freshener. Huck's presence had been expunged. Crawley expertly uncorked a bottle of Hector Bain's Wolf Blass chardonnay and poured a glass.

The contents of the roll were surprisingly fresh. He put his feet on the desk and sipped at the chilled, fragrant wine. The glossy apple was brown mush inside. He switched on the computer and responded to the prompt by typing in the terminal number. 'Come on, Boris,' he said. 'Give me something to do.'

Ruth May stared out at the lake from a window high in the National Library building. Around her were boxes of papers, folders filled with correspondence and photographs, loose-leaf binders stuffed to breaking

14

point with documents of varying shapes and sizes. The job of cataloguing the personal papers of the soldier, sportsman, diplomat and novelist, Rory Michael Broderick, had fascinated her from the time she unfolded the first letter. It had been from one of his many mistresses and the stiff, creamy paper carried several small brown stains. These were drops of Lady Angela Dettering's menstrual blood, as she explained, indicating that she was not pregnant as she had feared. A pregnancy would have been highly inconvenient as Sir Bernard Dettering had been on an overseas posting for the past year. Broderick had made use of the incident in his best-selling novel, *The Cleaning of the Slate*.

Now these enticing materials lay unnoticed as Ruth grieved for her father and pondered the mystery of his death. She had loved her gentle, scholarly father deeply and was immensely grateful to him for passing on to her a love of books. Ruth's mother had died when she was twelve and Barry May had completed the job of raising his daughter with outstanding success. She had graduated with first class honours in history from the University of Melbourne, secured a similar result for her Master's thesis on the history of the Botanical Gardens. She had preceded her father to the ACT, qualifying as a librarian and securing a post at the National Library. For the short time Barry May had worked in Canberra, father and daughter had amicably shared a house in Curtin. But Ruth had applauded her father's decision to move to the south coast. He was tired and disenchanted and she, at twenty-six, felt a need to live alone and explore some of life's possibilities.

She reproached herself now. She was convinced that

her father had been murdered, probably as a result of making an unwise choice of some kind. She had always been on hand to discuss his choices, to point him in the direction of practicality and away from his habitual book-fed dreaming. But it was seeing the big shambling bald-headed man a few hours ago that had deepened her suspicions. He had been in the background at the funeral in Coota Coota two days before, and here he was again. Ruth had been walking in the gardens around the administration complex and had seen him hurrying from the FSA building. She had known that her father worked in a high security environment, but had imagined him as a librarian or archivist. Now she was not so sure.

She tore her eyes from the flat blue surface of the lake and tried to give her attention to the documents. But Broderick's philanderings and posturings, formerly so amusing, suddenly seemed absurd. She put on her glasses and looked impatiently at the series of photographs she had propped up on a shelf in front of her. They showed Broderick progressing from a cheeky, round-faced boy through his handsome youth and middle years to the very picture of grey-bearded Edwardian distinction.

'You old fraud,' she said. 'You bloody phoney.'

'Ruth? You okay?' Frank Hume, with whom she shared a cramped workspace, looked at her with surprise. He was an earnest man with thinning hair and a thickening body. A few years older than Ruth he was clearly interested in her, but he was not one of the possibilities Ruth was anxious to explore.

'I'm all right. Bit tired. I think I'll knock off early.'

'You look a bit whacked. I could pack it in as well and we could have a drink. Pick you up a bit.'

'Not today, thanks.' Ruth straightened the desk, locking away the back-up disk on which there was a copy of her emerging catalogue, and scooped up her bag. She nodded at Hume and left the room, striding on long slim legs, untidy black hair swirling.

'Dyke,' Hume muttered.

Ruth heard him and swung around. 'What?'

Colour suffused Hume's face and he bent over his work. 'Nothing.'

Why am I so aggressive all of a sudden? Ruth thought. *What's happening to me?*

She left the building, scarcely noticing the librarians, administrators and readers inside and the inevitable tourists gawking at the artwork and displays in the foyer. Ruth was tall, as her mother had been, and she had towered over her diminutive father from puberty onwards. She had strong features and a firm slender body which could have been described as athletic, except that Ruth May's hand–eye coordination was poor and she had never taken any interest in sport. Incongruously, she drove well, and her late model Pulsar was one of her few indulgences. She spent very little on clothes and her appearance, but usually managed to look striking in a somewhat accidental way. She had had numerous short-lived love affairs and was acutely aware of the difficulty she faced in this area—on one level she was attracted to gentle men like her father, on another she craved something different. Consequently, neither the rather lost, divorced academics nor the alcoholically inclined journalists and political functionaries lasted very long.

She drove from the carpark, enjoying the car's power, and planning to go around the lake with the sunroof open and the windows down, perhaps even risking a speeding fine. She needed some release and it was nothing Rory Broderick or Frank Hume could give her. A 2.5 litre motor and Pavarotti, both at full blast, might do the trick. She found herself weeping as 'Nessun dorma' boomed out and she took her foot from the accelerator. The Pulsar slewed right as it lost power and the driver behind her fought the wheel to get around it on a bend that was blind for most of the curve. Ruth saw his white, strained face as he went past and vicariously experienced his fear and anger.

'I'm sorry. Shit, I'm sorry,' she said, stabbing angrily at the cassette player buttons, killing the music. 'Jesus, Dad, you were supposed to die in bed at eighty-five.'

She drove the rest of the way sedately, in silence. The neat, sculptured suburb soothed her and she cruised up the cement driveway to the carport. The house was twenty-five years old, one of the first to be built in the area. Its lines were relaxed: constructed of Bessa bricks, it had big windows overlooking small courtyards and the front and back yards featured low-maintenance ground cover, pebbled areas and hanging ferns. Barry May had paid the deposit and left Ruth with low mortgage commitments. His superannuation payout had gone to buy his Coota Coota cottage outright, a property which was now hers. Ruth locked the Pulsar, setting the alarm, and tried to feel good about the modest, tasteful house. She couldn't do it. She wanted to pick up one of the polished stones and throw it through the nearest, biggest pane of glass. She stalked back down the drive to the letterbox, wrenched up the lid and grabbed the fistful of paper. Still more paper, most of it destined for the garbage bin.

It was very quiet in Curtin on a weekday in the late afternoon. Ruth May wanted to scream obscenities at the TV aerials and fire a gun into the pellucid air. She crunched along the crushed stone path in her medium heels up to the tiled porch. The door was made of solid wood and fitted with a sophisticated burglar alarm at Barry May's insistence. Ruth's key deactivated the alarm and allowed the first of the door locks to open. She used to find this procedure fun, now she was irritated by it. She withdrew the key, inserted it again and opened the door.

She stepped from quiet, ordered civility into wild, inchoate destruction.

~ 3 ~

Crawley's computer emitted a beep and he swung around to look at the screen. The message read, 'Activate mail function'. He knew how to do that much. Boris's communication, carrying his terminal code, was brief: 'Personnel files May & Hopkins deleted in computerisation process, 28/8/91. "A" class clearance required for requested records search. Advise. Exit.'

'Thanks for nothing,' Crawley said as he turned off the computer. Of course, it wasn't nothing—the deletion of the files of two former FSA members lately and puzzlingly dead was too striking to be dismissed as a coincidence. As for Huck's second request, a search for recently deceased agents, Crawley was disinclined to pursue the recommended course of seeking a top priority clearance. It meant making submissions to at least two committees and, possibly, no action until Bain's return from London. Crawley turned the computer on again and sent a request to Boris to investigate the present whereabouts of the hard, or paper, versions of the personnel files. He used the director's toilet and when he returned the response was there on the screen: 'Destroyed 27/8/91.'

Crawley was intrigued. An inveterate ignorer of memos and skipper of meetings, he had paid virtually no attention to the debate within the intelligence services over the culling of records, the releasing of information under the FOI act or the extension of the protection period from thirty to fifty years. He regarded it all as bureaucratic manoeuvring designed primarily to expand and protect empires and advance careers. He was aware that records had been culled but he doubted that the files of two relatively recently employed officers would be deemed redundant. There would be superannuation payments and other entitlements still well and truly current. More interesting were the dates—if Boris's information was correct, and Crawley had never known it not to be, the hard files on Hopkins and May were destroyed *before* they were deleted in the computerisation exercise.

Crawley was not much given to speculation or theorising, especially when he had few facts to work with, but the matter in hand appeared to invite it. Why would two archivists be physically removed? Obviously because they knew something dangerous to someone. Why would they also be removed administratively, as it were? Harder to answer. Almost as hard as to say what they might have known. Archivists, by definition, could know many things. For Crawley that left the most interesting and potentially exciting question of all: who was threatened?

He changed his mind and went through the laborious process of asking for a top priority clearance for a record of all FSA personnel who had died within the past six months. Carol Mainwaring, uncomfortable at dealing with a superior venturing unnecessarily out of his office in his stockinged feet, raised an eyebrow as Crawley signed the application.

'Interesting, eh, Carol?'

'Yes, sir.'

'Don't call me sir. You make me feel like an American. D'you happen to know anyone in Archives?'

'Well, yes. Several people, actually.'

'Anyone dating back to the Melbourne days?'

The secretary tapped a button putting an in-coming

phone call on hold. 'No, I don't think so. All younger people.'

'Who's the boss down there? Or is it *up* there?'

'Down. Dr Dacre.'

'Male or female?'

She smiled and for the first time Crawley found her attractive. Her thin lips relaxed and there was suddenly something sexy about her severe features. Crawley was reminded of Jamie Lee Curtis. *Careful, Ray*, he thought. *She'd give Hector Bain your dick measurement in millimetres.* 'Male, of course, Mr Crawley. Dr Rupert Dacre. There are absolutely no female senior executives in the FSA.'

'Mary Stuyvesant blew it for you,' Crawley said. 'Would you please get Dr Dacre on the telephone for me, Ms Mainwaring.'

'Yes, sir.'

Back in his office, Crawley reflected on the exchange and reminded himself about the danger signals. Some of the most hectic and destructive romantic entanglements he'd experienced had been with women he'd at first disliked. There was some kind of sexual charge set up by overcoming the antipathy. The trouble was that the dislike could resurface, painfully, in another guise, and all hell break loose. He and Mandy were on an even keel, giving and taking, mutually respecting each other's differences. If Mandy were being unfaithful to him she was discreet about it, a faculty Crawley had never developed. He didn't want to get between Carol's long thin thighs or explore the lean contours of her chest. He didn't need the grief.

The telephone jolted him from this heated self-analysis. 'Yes, Carol?' He realised that his voice was throaty.

'Dr Dacre on line three, sir.'

A brisk voice, private-school accented. 'Rupert Dacre, Mr Crawley. What can I do for you?'

Crawley had to refocus. *Why had he wanted to talk to this man?* He cleared his throat to gain time and picked up the thread. 'Just a matter of interest, Rupert. How many people have you got on the strength down there?'

Caution shaped the rounded vowels. 'I could find out precisely if you . . .'

'Ballpark figure.'

'I beg your pardon?'

'Roughly, Rupert, roughly—give or take a few.'

'About twenty-five.'

'Anyone there who was in archives when the agency was based in Melbourne? What about you?'

'Oh no, certainly not me. I was appointed two years ago on a five-year contract. I very much doubt if we have anyone of that . . . vintage.'

Fuck you. That's my vintage. 'What happened to them all? I seem to remember swarms of people down in a basement. Filing cabinets galore . . .'

The voice was confident again. 'Most took redundancy packages, I believe. A few made the move to Canberra and I'm told they were helpful in the transition to computer storage. But when that was completed they retired. There has been a major rationalisation. Contract employment is the rule now.'

'Do you remember a man named Barry May?'

A hesitation, perhaps. 'No. May I ask the reason for these inquiries, Mr Crawley? The director hasn't expressed any dissatisfaction with our services. Do you have a difficulty?'

Paranoid and afraid, Crawley decided. *There's definitely something going on here.* He assured Dacre

23

that his inquiry was merely routine, a matter of catching up with changes in the FSA environment. The jargon failed to comfort the archivist and he sounded troubled when Crawley ended the call. Absorbed now, Crawley thought back over what he had learned, probing for an entry into the subject that didn't involve computers and committees. If there was anything solid to be learned at Coota Coota, Huck would discover it. What about Launceston and Hopkins? Was there a way in there? His appraisal was interrupted by a soft knock at the door. Carol Mainwaring entered. She had taken off her suit jacket to reveal a silk blouse with a loose tie at the neck. Her shoulders, without the aggressive padding, looked surprisingly soft and her waist was tiny.

'Fax from Mr Bain,' she said, placing the document on the desk. 'It appears he will be delayed in London for another week.'

Crawley was about to accept the sign and make the move that the stars and planets, or perhaps the hormones, dictated. Then a thought struck him. *May's daughter—what was her name? Ruth. And she lives in Canberra*!

'Thank you, Ms Mainwaring,' he said.

Huck's flight left on time and encountered no delays in the short flight to Bega. He had left his Kombi van at the airport and, within minutes of the touchdown, he was driving south to Coota Coota. Crawley, he reflected, never changed—always sceptical, threatening to become abusive. Always prepared to come through for a mate. Seeing him in that poncy office had been a shock, though. Huck recalled the space he and Crawley had shared in Melbourne, scarcely room for an extra cockroach. He wondered what would happen to Crawley after he left the FSA. At other times it had looked as if Creepy would either be sacked or leave in a body bag, now he seemed likely to stay the distance. Huck found it hard to imagine him in quiet retirement. For all the antagonism between him and the institution, Crawley needed the FSA. The way things were going the FSA might be disbanded before Crawley got his retirement. It was all very confusing to Huck.

He made good time on the familiar road and experienced the usual lift in spirits when he came over the rise and saw the ocean. The subject of the name of the body of water was a long-standing talking point on the coast between Australians who insisted on the Pacific Ocean and Kiwis who preferred the Tasman Sea. Huck was a passionate Pacificist. Barry May had backed him up, arguing from a botanical point of view, but then Barry had been a sixth-generation Australian like himself. Huck realised how much he missed the quiet, humorous little man. He took the Coota Coota turn-off thinking that he should have spoken to Barry's daughter at the funeral. But she had looked composed whereas he was very upset and had feared saying the wrong thing.

A great many things bothered Huck about his friend's death, apart from the unlikelihood of a fishing accident. May was a strong swimmer and the sea had been calm throughout the time between when he had last been seen and the discovery of his body. A non-smoker, light drinker and energetic walker, May had been fit with no history of heart trouble or other physical weakness. As men in their fifties will, Huck and May had discussed their health, and Huck, the pipe

25

smoker and reformed boozer, had felt himself to be the greater actuarial risk. But it was the manner of the death that nagged at him most. Death by drowning was easy to contrive if you knew what you were doing. Huck had pulled it off himself more than once.

He drove through the permanently open gate, locked into place by ancient, rusted hinges, and up the rutted track beside his weatherboard cottage. The building had been shaped by the coast winds and had settled comfortably into the landscape like an oddly moulded dune.

Huck lifted his overnight bag from the seat and whistled for his dog. Toby, a German Shepherd, would wait for the whistle, even though he recognised the vehicle. He came racing from the scrub behind the house, ears back, clearing a fallen log like a steeplechaser. Huck let the dog lick his face.

'I'll dump the bag, mate. Then we'll go over to Barry's. Might get a rabbit on the way, eh?'

Fifteen minutes later he was standing outside Barry May's house, a fibro and iron structure on brick pillars that Huck had helped install to replace the original wooden stumps. This was the only renovation May had attempted, and Huck was saddened when he remembered how well they'd worked together on the job. The house was set well back from the beach but sand still drifted into the garden and sea spray limited the kinds of plants that would survive. May had found this interesting and had begun experimenting with different species of shade trees, protective shrubs and ground covers. There were hundreds of plants in plastic pots, wilting now after a few days' neglect.

Huck went down the path to the back of the house where a rickety veranda was enclosed with fibro sheets, louvre windows and a warped door. It was the sort of place Huck could break into with his eyes closed. He patted the dog and ran some water into a bowl Barry had kept by the back step for this purpose. 'Hang on here, sport. I'm going inside for a look-see.'

The lock on the buckled door yielded to a knife blade and a push. Huck entered, took off his cap, leaned his .22 against the wall and went quickly through the house, assessing the degree of disturbance since he had last been there. At a guess, the daughter had been through, moving a book here, examining a photograph there. She had evidently made a cup of tea and emptied out the refrigerator, the door of which stood open. Otherwise the place was essentially the way Barry had left it—neat, minimally furnished and dominated by books. One of the two bedrooms had been used as a study and would be the focus of Huck's attention. There was a steel filing cabinet and a desk with several drawers. Huck knew what he would be looking for—Barry's diary and any document that appeared to connect with his former life.

Before he could face the search he needed a drink. Barry kept a modest supply in the kitchen and Huck went back there, picked up a glass from the draining board and bent to open the cupboard. As he did so he heard Toby growl and scratch once at the ground. He knew the dog was lying flat, alerted and watching. Huck peered through a dusty louvre pane towards the scrub behind the house but couldn't see anything. Toby was out of his line of sight under the house. He picked up the .22, released the safety catch and opened the back door, pressing himself against the jamb inside. Toby continued to growl. Huck located the sound. The dog was under the house and, at a guess, the sound that was alarming him was coming from the scrub.

Huck waited and Toby stopped growling. *Just a bush walker*, Huck thought, *or a local out for a stroll.* He stepped through the door onto the top step and bent to make eye contact with . . . Two shots boomed out in quick succession and glass, fibro and weathered timber broke and shattered, showering shards and splinters over Huck's bald head.

~ 4 ~

Rupert Dacre's palm was sweating when he hung up after speaking to Crawley. A fastidious man, he took a tissue from a box on his desk, wiped the moisture away and dropped the crumpled tissue into the waste paper bin. He leaned back in his chair and let his gaze wander around his office. How different things were now from twenty years ago, he reflected. Back then an archivist could expect to see living documents in his office—a manuscript diary or letters, a minuted typescript draft of a speech or report. Now it was all CD Rom storage and microfiche indexes, faxes and xeroxes. But Dacre had sniffed the wind as a young archivist and had wangled himself a scholarship to the United States where he had acquired all the latest knowledge about electronic storage and retrieval. He had gained a doctorate in the area and, on returning to Australia, had set up a consulting business, which thrived as computers took their grip on every aspect of Australian public and private life.

His nervousness now was the result of lying to Crawley who, he had been told, was a bad man to cross. It was true that Dacre's appointment as head of the FSA archival section was only two years old, but his consultancy firm had been directly involved in the computerisation of the agency's records. Dacre had personally supervised much of the process and it became known that he had handled the task 'with sensitivity'. This had led to his being approached with the offer of a five-year contract. Under its terms, Dacre could retain his consultancy activities. He could expand them, in fact, because the position within the

FSA offered many congruent opportunities. Dr Dacre's duties included the oversight of the FSA's responses to FOI requests, the culling of redundant records and 'other contingencies'.

One of his major tasks had been the preparation of the case for extending the period of protection to fifty years. He could justifiably claim to have constructed a strong case and to have presented it with force and subtlety. The tide of opinion was running against the secret-keepers, however, and Dacre was aware that, if the submission failed, he would be called upon for more than sensitivity. Ruthlessness might be a better description. Damage-control measures had already been adopted and more were in progress. His conversation with Crawley formed part of the plan. Dacre, Hector Bain and Derek Ramsay, the director of the Bureau of National Assessment, were the only people alive who knew that the computerisation of the FSA's documents had been a very selective operation. The greater part of the records from the agency's early years remained in original paper and card form only, and throughout there were major discrepancies, carefully concealed by Dacre, between the computerised holdings and the original archives.

Dacre put through a call to Ramsay. The BNA chief suggested they meet over a drink at the Yarralumla Bridge and Social Club where both were members. Dacre was a passionate bridge player, renowned for his bold bidding and flamboyant play—incongruous behaviour in an otherwise sedate and proper man. He dealt with the few matters needing his attention and left his office. His identity card took him past the security precautions—X-ray screening, bag inspections, metal detectors—that were the norm for other archive officers. Usually Dacre enjoyed these privileges, like the reserved space in the underground carpark and the Ford Fairmont and mobile phone, all debited to the tax-payers, but today he took no pleasure in them. He drove to the club and found himself ordering a double scotch and ice with some urgency. Normally an occasional social drinker, he gulped the whisky down and ordered another. He had hoped and prayed that all this would not be necessary. He raised his glass and the memory of Crawley's harsh, mocking voice made his hand shake. All his life Rupert Dacre had tried to make up in intelligence what he lacked in physical courage. Often he would have traded some of the former for more of the latter.

'Rupert, you're getting well ahead of me.' Derek Ramsay was of medium height, like Dacre, but much more heavily built with an overstrong handshake. Dacre winced as the pressure constricted his fingers. Ramsay had arrived before Dacre and watched the archivist for a few minutes before showing himself— an old trick, but still a useful one. He had not expected Dacre, whom he thought of as an ambitious cold fish, to show signs of strain so early. The man's hand was unpleasantly moist. Ramsay ordered two drinks, signed the chit and took command, steering Dacre towards a quiet corner. The deep leather armchair seemed to swallow Dacre's thin frame. Ramsay relaxed into his chair and lit a cigarette.

'He rang,' Dacre said.

'Ah.'

'He wanted to know how long I had been head of archives and whether there were any employees dating back to when the agency was in Melbourne.'

'Of course. Good. Well, that all sounds very

satisfactory. How would you assess his attitude, Rupert?'

Dacre finished his second drink and stared at the fresh one Ramsay had bought. 'I'd call it threatening.'

Ramsay puffed smoke. 'Better get used to it, old chap. That's Ray Crawley, I'm afraid.'

Basic personal details on all State and Commonwealth public servants and academics were on the joint intelligence services data base and Crawley ran a check on Ruth May on the reasonable assumption that a librarian working in Canberra would be on file. The assumption was confirmed and he read the entry without enthusiasm. The woman sounded dull. He rang the National Library and was informed that Ms May had left early. The voice of the man answering the extension had dripped curiosity.

'May I ask who's calling? Do you want to leave a message?'

Crawley said, 'No,' and hung up. He consulted the data base manual and laboriously accessed the graphics file. Ruth Fenimore May's passport photograph appeared on the screen of the colour monitor.

'Jesus Christ,' Crawley said. He stared at the image, blinked in case he'd suffered some kind of brainstorm, and looked again. No mistake. Ruth May bore a startling resemblance to his wife. Mandy was a youthful-looking forty-three who made up expertly and took care of her appearance. Lighten Ruth May's hair and add ten years, although she was actually fifteen years Mandy's junior, and the two women could be sisters. He had made a note of the home address and phone number and put through a call. The result was a blizzard of sound. Crawley swore and instructed Carol Mainwaring to check the number with Telecom. He was advised that the connection registered as 'damaged'.

The secretary made no attempt to impede Crawley as he strode from the office, shrugging into his jacket and slapping his pockets to locate his keys. She made a note of the time below the list of the visitors Crawley had received and the telphone numbers he had called. She felt sure that Derek Ramsay would be interested in Graeme Arthur Huck and the abortive call to the Curtin number. The VDT in the director's office had been specially adjusted to monitor all usage and relay it to Carol Mainwaring's terminal. When she was sure that Crawley had left the building she tapped in the codes and called up the electronic mail he had received and the files he had accessed.

She made printouts of the enigmatic messages from Boris Stein and ran her eye over the Ruth Fenimore May file. A librarian. What possible ambition could a librarian have? What measure of power could such a person aspire to? Carol Mainwaring's knife-like features compressed malevolently as she looked at the photograph of the subject. *The hair's a mess*, she thought, *and she looks older than me*! She didn't like to be reminded of her age and the distance she still had to travel within the power structure. She activated the print function angrily. 'What a frump!' she whispered.

Crawley drove rapidly through the thin afternoon traffic. The ease of getting around by car was one of the attractions of living in Canberra. As he got older he found Sydney's congested roads more and more difficult to cope with, although he was still beguiled by the prospect of living in the city and not infrequently mentioned it to Mandy. Her response was less enthusiastic and he sometimes wondered if retirement from the FSA might mean the loss of his wife. Perhaps that was one of the reasons he had rejected the enticing early retirement options that came his way regularly.

His old, unwashed BMW, its red duco faded to a primer pink, looked shabby in the smartly tailored streets of Curtin. Crawley pulled up outside Ruth May's house and looked it over with a practised eye. The place was about the size he and Mandy needed now that their son and daughter had apparently left the nest for good. It had an unfussy, easily maintained look. Crawley walked up the path and knocked on the door.

'Yes? Who are you? What do you want?'

For Crawley, this was getting weirder by the minute. The woman standing in front of him was uncannily like his wife. Mandy on holiday, say, in jeans and a T-shirt, with her hair uncombed and no make-up. The thing that most rocked Crawley was the similarity in voice tone and body language. She stood and spoke aggressively, with the precise Melbourne female voice that hits consonants and vowels that are typically drawled in the country and slurred north of the Murray River. Although he had never laid eyes on her before, Crawley felt he knew this woman. He fumbled for the card that identified him, somewhat vaguely, as an officer of the department of the attorney general.

'Miss Ruth May? My name is Crawley. I'm a former colleague of your father's.'

'Is that a fact? And what does that make you?' Ruth snatched the card and looked at it. 'Damn it. I need my glasses.'

Crawley, the old campaigner, moved in physically

and verbally as she went on the back foot. 'I'd like to talk to you. Could we go inside? I tried to telephone but your line's dead. Have you had some trouble here?'

'No. I mean, I suppose so. Look, why are you here?'

Crawley could sense the distress undermining her purposefulness. He took her by the elbow and gently turned, steering her back into the house. Ruth retreated, still holding the card. Two steps inside the door, Crawley saw the beginnings of the destruction. A potted fern had been swept from its stand and the plant and soil had been trodden into the carpet. A framed abstract painting at the end of the passage hung skew-whiff behind shattered glass. Ruth shook herself free and walked away into the first room on the right. Crawley followed, almost flinching as he saw how alike her movements were to Mandy's.

'Take a look at this, whoever you are. It's a bloody shambles.'

The study resembled a junkyard, except that the debris had been new, well-cared for and intact possibly only hours ago. Academic journals were broken at the spine and ripped apart; chair upholstery was torn; a bookcase had been toppled, scattering the contents which had then been walked over; a metal filing cabinet was a twisted ruin. Ruth May picked up a pair of spectacles from the desk, onto which the contents of the drawers had been emptied, and examined Crawley's card.

'You wouldn't be from the FSA, would you, Mr Crawley?'

Crawley stared at her. 'Why d'you say that?'

Ruth shrugged. 'I've got a feeling that's who's behind all this.'

Crawley set a collapsed cane chair upright and

looked at the nearest of the wildly strewn books—
Oliver Sacks' *Seeing Voices; The Playmaker* by Thomas
Keneally; *The Whitlam Government 1972–1975* by
the great man himself. He had heard of each and read
none, a common experience. The shelves at home were
crammed with books he had dipped into but hadn't
had the patience to finish.

'I know your telephone's damaged. Is the rest of the
house like this?'

'Pretty much.'

'It's not a professional job.'

'You *are* a bloody spook. I knew it. Get out of here!'

Wearing glasses, Ruth May looked less like Mandy
and Crawley felt marginally more comfortable. He
reclaimed his card. 'It's not as easy as that. You've
made a serious allegation against a branch of the
security services.'

'I withdraw it. This was all done by Muslim fanatics
who know I eat pork chops for breakfast seven days
a week.'

Crawley grinned. He decided that he liked this
woman. 'You need some help, Ms May. I can get your
phone fixed and all this cleaned up. I can smooth the
way with the insurance people and arrange to have the
house guarded.'

'In return for what?'

'A frank talk . . .' Crawley noticed that Ruth was
shaking. She had lost colour and seemed to be about
to collapse. He moved closer to her and she steadied
herself defensively. 'I want to talk to you about your
father and his work and just about anything else you're
willing to talk about.'

Ruth did not answer. She was staring at a
photograph that had been torn from its frame. The

face in the picture had been distorted by its being crumpled but Crawley experienced again the shock of recognition, as if he knew the subject in her fifties suit and hat. 'My mother,' she said. 'Bastards.'

'You look like you need a drink,' Crawley said. 'Got anything strong in the house?'

'If they haven't broken it. You might as well come through, since I can't get rid of you. I suppose you'd have done your worst by now if you were going to. Jesus, I don't understand any of this.'

'Neither do I,' Crawley said. 'That's why we have to talk. Why do you think the FSA's involved?'

He followed her down the passage past another wrecked room, through a sitting room that had been scarcely disturbed to a scene of devastation in the kitchen. Ruth pointed. 'There's the phone connection, if you're interested.'

The jack had been ripped from the wall; the plastic coating had peeled back, exposing the wires. Ruth opened a cupboard and took out a half full bottle of Dewar's scotch. 'My dad used to drink this.'

Crawley took the bottle. He found two glasses on the draining board and poured generous measures. Then he ran some water into each glass. 'About the FSA . . .'

Ruth looked warily at her drink, then she rubbed at her calf where she'd cut it against an upturned filing cabinet. She'd stopped the blood flow with cotton wool and covered the deep cut with an Elastoplast, but it was itching. 'There's this big man. I saw him at the funeral in Coota. A thuggish type with a bald head and daggy clothes. I saw him again today coming out of the FSA building.'

Crawley nodded and sipped his scotch.

~ 5 ~

Toby's loud barking and the sound of a car engine assured Huck that he was still alive. He could feel blood trickling from his lacerated scalp and the vision in one eye was blurred. Despite his bulk, he jumped from the top step onto the grass, yelled to Toby to show himself and ran towards the scrub. He knew that the road down to the back of Barry May's house was steep and rough and that he might get a glimpse of the vehicle. Toby caught up in a few leaps and trotted alongside, still barking. Huck crashed through the trees until he reached a point with a view of the road. He blinked and wiped at his bleary eye. Above him and 200 metres away he saw the tail end of a blue car, expertly navigating the ruts, topping the rise, throwing up dust.

Huck looked disgustedly at the pea rifle in his grip. 'Clint Eastwood'd have a shot,' he said.

Toby stopped barking. Huck put his hand up and felt the blood on his head. He rubbed it off on the sleeve of his shirt and felt the glass slivers in the material. Barry May had no near neighbours. The sound of the shots had disturbed no one and the sandy little patch returned quickly to its usual tranquillity. Huck trudged back to the cottage, stripped off his shirt and cleaned himself up in the outhouse bathroom. The cuts were not serious and he stopped the oozing blood with a few wads of toilet paper soaked in methylated spirits.

He climbed the steps and examined the damage caused by the shots. It had been a heavy calibre weapon with a fairly rapid rate of fire, operated at a reasonably close range. Huck concluded that the shooter had not tried to kill him but had fired high with great accuracy. The realisation did not comfort him. He re-entered the kitchen, located the bag of dry food Barry had kept for Toby and poured some into the dog's bowl.

'Have a feed and keep your eyes open,' he said.

Huck prided himself on his skill at locating hiding places in the houses of civilians. He went about it systematically, working from the most likely spots towards the more ingenious. As he would have anticipated, Barry May's hidey-hole fell in the middle range. Floor boards creaked under a carpet square in the main bedroom with a different sound from the give in the floor in other parts of the house. Huck peeled back the carpet and found where a section had been cut through and slotted back into place. He lifted the boards clear and found a plastic-wrapped package taped to the underside of the joist.

'Not bad, mate,' Huck said. 'Not bad at all.'

He lifted the package clear and put everything back the way it had been. A feeling of unease crept up his spine and he wanted to be out of the house. He and May had never spoken much about intelligence work and the FSA. It had been as if this bond between them didn't need renewing, almost as if their friendship depended on ignoring it. Huck disliked exercising his old skills in his friend's house, even if it was in an attempt to throw light on Barry's puzzling death. Professional that he was, he continued his search but he found no other concealment. He left the house, slamming the door back into its broken frame and achieving a reasonable closure. He whistled Toby out of the scrub where he was sniffing rabbit droppings, and walked back across country and along a stretch of rocky beach to his own house with the .22 over his shoulder, his cap stuffed in a pocket and the plastic bundle under his arm.

Although he had had only one drink, Crawley drove from Curtin to his house in Weston as if he was drunk. He could not concentrate on the traffic flow or road signs, and several times felt he was failing to control the BMW on the bends. He gripped the steering wheel, shook his head and tried to regain a measure of control and objectivity. It was a cruel thing to happen to a man—to meet up with a younger, vulnerable replica of his wife, and feel, with deep urgency and immediate force, emotions that belonged properly and safely in the past.

He switched on the radio and let the news broadcaster's voice bounce around inside the car. He absorbed nothing of the reports beyond a vague sense that things were bad and getting worse. He turned the radio off after the weather report, which had not registered. At his age, Crawley reflected, he should be insulated against hormonal disturbances flooding through his system like power surges on an electricity supply grid. He was too old to be coping with images of Carol Mainwaring with her matt complexion, razor features and flat chest. Crawley sang in a passable imitation of John Lennon:

I've gotta girl named Boney Maroni
She's as skinny as a stick of macaroni . . .
He recalled the Sinatra song, too:
My lean baby, she's so wan
When she stands sideways you think she's gone . . .
Crawley was well aware that he only sang when he was happy, so why was he singing now? There was

nothing to be happy about—certainly not at the image of Ruth May, grimacing as she drank her whisky but getting it down, and denouncing a man whose description perfectly matched that of Huck as the intruder who had vandalised her house. The accusation unsettled Crawley quite as much as his powerful attraction to the woman. Could Huck be working some devious game of his own? Crawley could almost discount the idea—*almost*! Huck's agendas and his had usually coincided, but he was conscious that Barry May's death had affected Huck deeply.

He entered the pleasant tree-lined street, slowed, turned right and ran up beside the house. He slewed left at the end of the driveway. The carport, by common agreement, was reserved for Mandy's car, not because the vehicle was more worthy of care—it was a battered Honda Civic—but because Mandy, who was a poor driver, preferred to back straight out. In the depleted Crawley household it was usually Mandy who left first, fresh after an abstemious evening, and ever eager to do battle with her bureaucratic enemies.

The Honda Civic was in its slot. His wife of almost twenty-four years was at home. Crawley entered the house feeling a combination of puzzlement, guilt and excitement.

'Hello, darling.' Mandy looked up from the *Canberra Times*, which she read in the evening after reading the specially delivered Melbourne *Age* in the morning.

Crawley bent and kissed her cheek, smelling the lingering odours of her day—air-conditioned offices, hers and other women's perfumes, aftershave, cigar smoke and deceit. 'Hello, love. What's new?'

'What's new is old stuff,' Mandy said crisply. 'I've

been dying for a drink but I waited for you. Aren't I good?'

'You are,' Crawley said. 'I'll have whatever you're having and line up another one ready.'

Mandy went to the kitchen and made two stiff gin and tonics, going easy on the mixer and ice. She brought the drinks back to where Crawley was slumped in a chair.

'Are you all right, Ray? I mean, I can't ask for details, but the way things are there can't be any real difficulties, can there?'

Crawley accepted the glass, swilled it around and took a long pull. 'You mean I'm redundant.'

'I didn't say that.'

The solid injection of alcohol, on top of the emotion, inflamed him. 'That's what you meant.'

Mandy sipped her drink. 'I don't want to fight tonight, Ray. I've got too much to do.'

'Does the surname May mean anything to you, sweetheart?'

'No. Should it?'

'How about . . .' Crawley searched his disturbed and distressed memory for the word and homed in on it like an eager dance partner. 'Fenimore?'

'Yes, of course. Ray . . .'

'Come on, love, humour me.'

'It's my mother's maiden name.'

'I thought it was Ross or something like that.'

'Mum was married briefly to a man named Rose before she met Dad. It was a sort of teenage thing, I gather. Anyway, her maiden name was Fenimore.'

'Jesus. She must be your bloody cousin or something.'

'Who? I'm getting a bit tired of this.'

'Yeah. I'm sorry. Look, did your mother have any sisters?'

'Ray, I know you've never been the least bit interested in my family, particularly my mother's side. But, yes—Mum has three sisters, my aunts, obviously.'

'D'you reckon one of them could've married a bloke named May?'

'The youngest one, Sally, ran away from home when she was a teenager, I don't know what happened to her, no one does. I never met her. Mum was fond of her. She said they looked alike.'

'She was right,' Crawley said. 'I saw a photo of her today. She looked like Lois must have before she got heavily into the cream buns.'

Crawley made two more drinks and told Mandy about his meeting with Ruth May and a little of the background to it. He usually avoided giving Mandy anything but the barest details of his working life— her relatively recently acquired radicalism had made her dismissive of his occupation, even more dismissive than Crawley was of her academic concerns. But this was different—a family matter almost. Mandy listened and was excited, although her excitement was tempered by a tone in Crawley's voice.

'Younger than me, you say? And darker? Do you want to fuck her, Ray?'

'Who are you fucking at the moment?'

Mandy set her glass down and pushed back some strands of her honey blonde hair, in which touches of grey were just beginning to show. 'Is this where we are? Again?'

'You tell me.'

Mandy's gorge rose; the idea of having to account for her life to a man was something she had rejected.

But they had been together for so long, survived so much that sometimes, for all Crawley's aggressive masculinity, she felt the gender barrier between them had broken down and that they were partners in a sense that feminist theory had never covered. 'I'm not fucking anyone else, and I don't particularly want to.'

Crawley smiled. 'Good,' he said. 'Your cousin is safe from me.'

Mandy sighed. He had manipulated her again, the way he had so many times before. She could feel herself getting angry and fought the impulse down. She *did* have too much on her plate to embark on a night of recrimination and confrontation, whether or not it ended well or badly. The telephone saved her from having to respond.

She came back looking amused. 'It's Huck,' she said. 'He tries so hard to be polite these days and he dislikes me so much.'

Crawley squeezed her arm as he went past. 'Huck doesn't dislike you. He just doesn't know how to take you. And he isn't the only one.'

'Fried rice. All right?'

'With red wine,' Crawley said. 'Plenty of red wine.'

'Hucky?'

'There's something up, Creepy. I got shot at today.'

'Shit, are you all right? What happened?'

Mandy raised an eyebrow at Crawley's tone. She brought his drink through to him and Crawley nodded his thanks as he listened to Huck's account of his activities.

Huck said, 'I found a package that contained a bunch of file cards—old style, the sort of thing I haven't seen for years. What're they called?'

'You mean punch cards?'

44

'Yeah, like that, but that's not the word. They've got bits nipped out down the sides and . . . perforations. That's it—perforated cards.'

'They must go back forty years.'

'Looks that way. What do you make of it? Do you know anyone who understands those things?'

'Boris might. You'd better shoot them up to me. Not to the depot though.'

'I can probably find someone to make the run tonight. Your place? Might be pretty early in the morning.'

'Doesn't matter,' Crawley said. 'Take care of yourself.'

'What've you been doing?'

'Talking to Barry May's daughter. She doesn't like the look of you, mate. Saw you at the funeral the other day and in Canberra this morning. She reckons you tossed her house today.'

'How could I? Did you tell her . . .'

'I didn't tell her anything. Maybe between her and Boris we can find out what the hell's going on here.'

~ 6 ~

Rupert Dacre looked across his desk at Boris Stein who sat awkwardly in his chair. Boris looked awkward in almost every situation other than installed in front of the keyboard. He twisted his feet under him and his fingers clenched and unclenched nervously.

'Mr Stein,' Dacre said, 'you are, I believe, a close associate of Ray Crawley's?'

'N-not exactly,' Boris said. 'Worked with him in Melbourne and up here, but . . .'

'Exactly. You've worked with him and you still do. I understand you performed some little tasks for him the other day. Freelance work, was it?'

'No. Official, of course.'

'Don't dissemble, Mr Stein. You bypassed archival procedures and accessed material directly. I know all about your skills. I was hoping to use them one day. How is your research on the mirror-image project going?'

Boris was startled out of his discomfiture. The mirror-image idea was his pet project. It involved the duplication of computerised records and the implantation codes which could be used to protect them and provide misinformation to, and identify unauthorised users of, the files. Boris was convinced that he could win computer immortality if he could perfect the program.

More confidently, he said. 'Still a few bugs yet, Dr Dacre.'

'Rupert, please. I'm very, very interested.' Dacre discussed some of the intricacies of the electronic information and retrieval world, sufficiently to impress Boris with his grasp. 'We'd like to help. I imagine you could do with more main-frame time, equipment, other things?'

'Certainly,' Boris said. As he spoke his confidence ebbed away. This had something to do with Crawley and that always meant trouble.

'Your cooperation is required,' Dacre said. 'Crawley will approach you with a request. I would be obliged if you would respond as I direct.'

Boris shook his head. 'I don't know. Crawley's a dangerous man to fool with. I . . .'

Dacre smiled. 'This request should properly come from Hector Bain, but he's overseas, as you know. I can get an authority from him within twenty-four hours, but things have moved faster than we expected. It is imperative that you act now.'

'Now?'

'Crawley will approach you today.'

Boris was divided: fear of Crawley warred with ambition, his *sole* ambition—to develop the mirror-image project. And that was for the long-term good of the FSA, surely? A more important consideration than the interests of one man. 'Can I get an assurance from you of support for my research?'

'Give me an outline of what you want. I'll write a directive today and forward it to the appropriate committee.'

'And you'll get an endorsement of your . . . request from the director?'

Dacre nodded. 'Tomorrow. Relayed to you. Coded and secure.'

'What if Crawley finds out?'

'He won't. And what you're going to tell him is the truth anyway. All you are doing is . . . expediting matters.'

'That's very mysterious.'

'The way it should be in this business, Mr Stein. Don't you think?'

Ruth May had accepted Crawley's offer of help to get her house cleaned up and restored. She told him that she had been thinking of selling the place for some time and that the death of her father and now this intrusion had accelerated the process. As she spoke she realised that all this was true but she hadn't realised it. She disliked the house with its neat suburban conformity. She didn't want to live in it a day longer. To her surprise she found herself admitting this to Crawley and almost going on to state her dissatisfaction with her job, her life. She pulled back from that, allowed him to book her a room in the Lake Royal hotel and agreed to meet him the next day. He helped her to open the jammed door of the closet where she kept an overnight bag and left.

As she packed the bag, Ruth was troubled by the way she had almost gone into confessional mode with a man she'd never met before. Why? True, the way he looked at her was unsettling, but there was more to it than that. He had a forcefulness she found attractive, why not admit it? He had barged in and told her virtually nothing, but here she was doing more or less as he instructed, trusting him. She became angry and, normally a meticulous and organised packer, she threw things heedlessly into the bag, plundering the resources of the vandalised house. She came across things she had treasured broken and abused and was indifferent. The desecration of books, which could have been expected to reduce her to tears, left her unmoved. *I've changed*, she thought as she slammed the door. *Why and into what?*

As she drove she had the feeling that he was watching her. She had an eye for cars, tried to remember what models had been parked in the street and couldn't recall a colour or shape. Was that him in the green Datsun, or in the white Merc or the red BMW? She laughed. Of course it wasn't him, and if he had been following her she wouldn't see him if he knew his business. Isn't that what they said? Who said? *Christ almighty. I'm going nuts!* She knew what she'd do: the Lake Royal was a fancy hotel. She'd have a long soak in their bath oil and wash her hair using their shampoo and conditioner. Then she'd drink some gin from the mini-bar and have a big dinner, putting it all on the FSA tab. She remembered throwing, for no earthly reason, a good dress and some fashionable shoes into the bag. She might meet a dark, handsome stranger.

She drove over the bridge and took the turn towards the hotel. She thought, *He's dark, he isn't handsome, but he certainly is strange!* The booking-in procedure went smoothly and Ruth began to relax and she enjoyed the unaccustomed pleasure of making a living area thoroughly untidy. She had a long, strong gin and tonic, soaked and luxuriated in the bath, and dressed and made up carefully. When she had finished she looked at herself in astonishment. It had been years since she had taken so much trouble over her appearance. Usually she ran a comb through her hair, applied a little lipstick and eye shadow and was out the door, more concerned about the cards on her desk than the clothes on her back. The woman she saw in the hotel mirror was striking—big-eyed, high-cheekboned, full-lipped. She flicked soapy water at the mirror. 'Liar,' she said.

She went down to the bar where she had another, milder, drink, and through to the restaurant. Her eating habits, in imitation of her father's, were erratic. She frequently skipped breakfast and seldom ate lunch. She was inclined to pick at nuts or potato chips through the day when hunger struck, and often the evening meal was virtually her first real food of the day. The menu reminded her that she had eaten very little since getting back from the funeral. Her appetite sharpened by alcohol and emotion, she was ravenous and ordered three substantial courses and a bottle of riesling. The restaurant was scarcely half full and the service was rapid. Ruth ate heartily, consuming more than half of the wine and only flagging when she reached the dessert. Fatigue flooded through her and she almost sagged in her seat. She pushed the chocolate mousse away and called for the bill. She signed it and put a five dollar note on the tray, stood steadily with an effort of will and stepped away from the table.

The waiter moved towards her. 'Are you all right, madam?'

'Perfectly,' Ruth said. She walked from the restaurant to the elevators, controlling the impulse to lean against the wall while she waited. Her eyes were closing, the rarely worn shoes were pinching and she had an urgent need for the toilet. *Some romantic dinner*, she thought. *If a man approached me now I'd piss all over him.* She stepped into the lift and rode it up to her floor. Outside her door she kicked off the shoes and fumbled in her bag for the key.

'Miss May?'

The small man had approached silently.

Ruth said, 'Yes,' as she slipped the key into the lock.

She was aware of a sudden movement and then only of a smell. She remained conscious long enough to associate it with a distant memory which she couldn't quite recall. Then she was weightless and drifting away into a dark enveloping void.

'She's not here?' Crawley snarled. 'What the hell do you mean she's not here?'

'I'm sorry, sir,' the receptionist said. 'I began calling her room when you phoned half an hour ago. There was no answer and there's still no response. What do you want me to do?'

Three minutes later Crawley, accompanied by the hotel's worried security manager, was turning the key in Ruth May's door. He strode into the empty room, opened the bathroom and pushed back the shower recess door.

'She *was* here,' the security man said. 'But she didn't sleep in the room.' He opened the built-in wardrobe and stepped back to stand helplessly. 'Maybe she . . . met someone.'

The suggestion enraged Crawley. He swept his expert eye over the untidy surfaces—no handbag, an almost empty glass, no way to guess at her intentions. 'It's ten o'clock, for Christ's sake.'

'It happens.'

'You're going to have to contact every room with a person still in it. I want to know about phone calls in and out and I'm going to have to talk to the night staff.'

The security man shook his head. 'We've got some very important people staying here. They'll scream blue murder. And I can't disrupt the running of the hotel like that.'

'Yes, you can,' Crawley said.

By 11 a.m. Crawley was satisfied that he had learned everything possible about Ruth May's brief stay in the hotel except the most important things—how, when and why she had left it. Her car was still in the hotel carpark, so there was a likely further question—with whom had she left? From experience Crawley knew that spiriting a person away from a busy hotel was a job for an expert. The knowledge did not comfort him. He left the hotel and drove to the FSA building with Ruth May's belongings in his car. He reproached himself for not having kept a closer watch on her. Following her to the hotel had not been enough. *'You're losing it,'* he said. *'Two people dead and a house ransacked and Huck shot at. You should have known this was serious stuff.'*

He parked, moved grudgingly through the security procedures so beloved by Hector Bain, and went directly to Boris Stein's office.

'You again, Crawley. What now?'

Crawley was surprised at Boris's unaccustomed aggression. 'Sorry, mate. Busy, are you?'

Boris lifted one hand from the keyboard and waved at a bank of image-filled screens. 'Always. But that's never stopped you before. What's that you've got there?'

Crawley cleared away a pile of floppy disks near Boris's elbow and laid the cards in the space. 'Seen these things before?'

Boris sniffed and took a tissue from a box balanced on top of a monitor. 'Sorry, lousy cold. Of course. They're Holorith cards. Stone age stuff. So what?' He blew his nose loudly.

Crawley attributed Boris's brusqueness to the cold

52

and made allowances. 'Can you make any sense of them?'

Boris picked up one of the cards and examined it carefully. 'Well, they're system cards, obviously. I'd say part of an index at a guess.'

'What kind of an index?'

'That'd take some finding out without knowing the provenance. Have you got any idea where these cards came from? I mean, from an insurance company, or military records, or immigration files? All sorts of big and not so big organisations used them—libraries, hospitals, the police . . .'

Boris sneezed and dabbed at his nose with the soggy tissue. Crawley looked at the screens, disks and computer tapes that filled the room. 'Tell me, Boris, old son,' he said slowly, 'did the FSA ever use . . . what did you call them again?'

'Holorith cards.' Boris sneezed again and nodded.

'Was that a yes, or just a bloody sneeze?'

'We used them. Before my time, of course, and yours. Back in the fifties.'

'Let's say they're FSA cards, then. Would that make it easier?'

'I suppose so. All the data would have been computerised but there must be a code. I could access it and search through the networks to . . .'

Crawley laid his hand on Boris's narrow shoulder. 'I don't need the details, fascinating as they may be. Just get on to it and tell me what you can as quick as you can. Please.'

Boris dropped the wet tissue into the waste paper basket and pulled out another. 'You said please. This is important, is it, Crawley?'

Crawley suddenly had a mental picture of Ruth

May, standing stricken amid the shambles in her house. He was reminded of a fight he had with Mandy when he'd smashed a glass, overturned her brimming ashtray, woken the children in the early hours with his shouting. Mandy's face had worn the same expression. 'It could be, Boris,' he said. 'When d'you reckon you might have something for me?'

'If you get out of my hair now and everyone else leaves me alone, maybe later this afternoon.'

'Unplug your phone and skip lunch,' Crawley said. 'I'm running this show, remember. If anyone gives you trouble, put them straight onto me.'

Boris sneezed. 'Right.'

'Thanks. And Boris, none of this electronic mail bullshit. Come up and see me when you've got something. I'll give you some of Hector's Dimple Haig—be good for your cold.'

'I don't drink, Crawley. You know that.'

'Probably why you've got the bug. Never mind, I'll get Ms Mainwaring to make you a nice cup of tea.'

~ 7 ~

Carol Mainwaring had tracked Crawley's progress through the building. She waited for him outside his office, papers in hand, the model secretary. She wore a modified Vietnamese costume—high-necked white silk shirt coming down to her hips over wide black culottes. With her sharp features and rail-thin figure, the outfit was effective, suggesting something exotic, even possibly lubricious, to accompany the image of efficiency.

'Good morning, Mr Crawley. Rather a lot for you to attend to this morning, I'm afraid.'

'And I'm afraid I won't give it a glance, Carol. Why don't you establish a basket for Hector? You could call it the ECWD basket, how'd that be?'

Carol Mainwaring's pen flickered over the pad she somehow managed to juggle along with the faxes and other documents. She looked expectantly at Crawley and noticed with distaste his partial shave and ill-buttoned, well-worn denim shirt. 'And what would that signify, Mr Crawley?'

'Everything Crawley wouldn't do.' He pushed past her and paused before closing the door. 'That's a nice outfit, Carol. Just bring me in the absolute essentials, eh? I need some elbow room today.'

Carol Mainwaring retreated, fuming, to her desk. She slammed the papers down and fumbled in her bag for a cigarette before she remembered the smoke-free workplace rules. This did not improve her temper. She found a packet of Nicorettes and chewed one of the tablets vigorously. With a measure of composure restored, she assembled a few letters for Crawley's signature and took them into the office. He signed them without interest or comment. She returned to her desk and asked one of the clerks to fetch her a cup of coffee. She sipped the drink, gazing back at the shut door. An in-coming phone call she put automatically on hold. *God damn him*, she thought. *Think of yourself and get on with it*. She stabbed the buttons to call Rupert Dacre's extension.

'He's taken the bait, then?' Derek Ramsay said.

Rupert Dacre nodded. 'So it would seem. I'm told that he is in a somewhat agitated state, alternately aggressive and apologetic. From all I've heard, an excessively volatile Crawley is not something to be taken lightly.'

'Hold your nerve, Rupert. There are many things in prospect for you if all goes well.'

The two men were meeting in a small conference room in the intelligence services complex. There was a telephone on the table, a carafe of water and three glasses and a packet of polaroid photographs. These Ramsay fanned out for Dacre to look at. The archivist paled as he examined the prints.

'Was this really necessary?'

Ramsay chuckled. 'They were supposed to set your mind at ease. As you can see, the young woman has come to no harm and is being well treated.'

One of the photographs showed Ruth May apparently asleep on a narrow bed in an austere-looking room; in another she was sitting at a table eating a spartan breakfast of fruit, toast and coffee; a third shot showed her, dressed incongruously in an elegant black dress and cheap sneakers, walking in a small, walled-in garden. Dacre flicked back to the first picture. 'She's a librarian,' he said. 'For god's sake see that she gets something to read. Otherwise she'll go crazy.'

'Your acceptance and suggestion are duly noted,' Ramsay said dryly.

Dacre poured water and sipped nervously. 'I still don't like it. What about this other chap—Luck?'

'Huck. He's not your problem. When Crawley gets the information through Stein your role becomes crucial. Do you have confidence in Stein?'

Dacre lifted his glass from the polished surface of the table and looked at the ring it left behind. He obliterated the mark with the tip of his finger. 'He's a Jew, so of course he can spot and seize an advantage. The trouble with Jews is that they go on seeing and seizing advantages.'

Ramsay smiled. 'Noted, Rupert,' he said. 'And may I say I think you're beginning to get the feel of things.'

'Record-keeping is of the essence,' Dacre said. 'The first written records, the first *necessity* for written records, arose when tribute had to be paid and receipted. Religious tribute mostly, but . . .'

Ramsay raised his hand. 'I don't need the lecture. In the present climate everything to do with your branch of the intelligence services is of the utmost importance. No possible argument about that. You're in the box seat, Rupert. All you have to do is play your cards shrewdly. Don't be intimidated or . . . drawn by Crawley. Just give him what he wants and let him go. You wouldn't be a fly fisherman, by any chance?'

Dacre pushed his chair back and stood. 'No, Derek, I'm not. But I've read Hemingway and I know exactly what you're going to say next. So don't bother.' He walked from the room, satisfied, as one of his professors in Chicago had stressed as a requirement for executives, that he'd given as good as he'd gotten.

'Yes? Can I help you?' Carol Mainwaring challenged Boris Stein as he approached her desk. Boris was very nervous with sweat breaking out on his high, domed forehead. Women terrified him at the best of times, but this one, with her axe-blade nose and knife-slash mouth reminded him of pictures he had seen of hungry sharks. Instinctively, he began to speak in rapid Polish and to gesticulate in the direction of Crawley's door. The secretary drew back and Boris dashed past her. She saw her error and pursued him, culottes flapping, heels tapping on the carpet, but Boris got the door open before she caught him.

Crawley looked up expectantly as Boris almost fell into his office. The computer man slid along the wall as Carol Mainwaring came through the door.

'It's all right, Carol,' Crawley said. 'Dr Stein is a friend of ours.'

Boris dropped into a chair. 'You've never called me doctor before, Crawley.'

'First time for everything. What have you got for me? It better be good, Herr Doktor, or I'll turn you over to her and she's a killer.'

'How does Hector stand her?'

Crawley shrugged. 'I'd only be guessing. Come on, Boris, I've been sitting here on my arse all day. Give!'

Boris took a handkerchief from his pocket, sneezed, wiped his nose and then dried his forehead. Crawley looked away, feigning interest in a document on his desk. Boris sniffed deeply and held up three fingers, the nails of which were dirty. 'Three cards, right?'

'Boris . . .' Crawley said warningly.

'Okay. I was right. They were index cards relating to a master list of FSA operatives in the period 1950–59. I was able to work back through the encoding of the Holorith records. How's that?'

'Terrific,' Crawley said. 'And . . .'

'What do you want?'

'The names, for Christ's sake!'

'I want to do a deal with you, Crawley.' Boris snuffled into his handkerchief after speaking.

Crawley was astonished. He had worked with Boris Stein for almost fifteen years without the computer expert ever imposing conditions. Not a natural bully, Crawley had fallen into the habit of semi-bullying Boris in the sincere belief that this was what made him function effectively. Either he had been wrong from the start or something had changed; Crawley's senses all went simultaneously on the alert. 'A deal, Boris?'

'Leave me alone. After this, leave me alone to get on with my work. I'm sick of doing these little jobs for you. I . . . I've got bigger fish to fry.'

Bullshit, Crawley thought, *pure, unadulterated bullshit. And very interesting as such.* He smiled at Boris and straightened a paper clip. 'I'm hurt, Boris. I thought you liked being at the cutting edge occasionally. But, okay, if that's what you want. It's a deal.'

'The cards relate to two men and one woman— August Pope, Richard Beale and Beatrice Henderson.'

Crawley wrote the names on a pad. He waited for Boris to go on and when he heard nothing he looked up sharply. 'Yes?'

'That's it.'

'What the hell d'you mean, that's it? Are they real names or what? August Pope, I don't like the sound of that too much. I've never heard of these people. Were they on the strength, contract types, off-duty wallopers . . . ?'

Boris shrugged. His features contorted and he sneezed loudly. 'I don't have the faintest idea.'

'Did you try to find out?'

'Of course I did. I told you, I want you off my back. When I'd got the names I ran checks on them, pushing as hard as I could. I got absolutely nowhere.'

'Meaning?'

'Meaning that any further info on them is securely blocked and to get past those blocks you'll have to talk to Dr Dacre.'

~ 8 ~

Reggie Carmichael was a Coota Coota character, the local defective, ignored by most, tolerated by all. He spent most of his time on the wharf fishing but had never been known to catch anything. It was widely doubted that he used bait and even the presence of a hook was in some dispute. Reggie lived in a shed behind the town bowling club where he did odd jobs to supplement his pension. He had just enough wit to draw money from the bank and to wash and shave reasonably regularly. He had many eccentricities, among them a habit of memorising the registration numbers of motor vehicles not belonging to locals. The rough road in, and the rather gritty, rocky beaches deterred all but the most persistent tourists so that the number of strange cars around was never large. But Reggie's memory emptied out the data rapidly, so Huck went looking for him early on the morning following the shooting and after he had despatched the package to Crawley.

Reggie was not on the wharf or in his shed or picking leaves from the bowling green. Huck found him wandering along the beach road deftly knocking an empty can ahead of him with a stick.

'Gidday, Reg.'

Reggie hit the can five metres. 'Gidday.'

'Busy?'

'Yeah, busy. That's right. Yeah.' The can sailed another five metres and landed upright on a stone. A perfect lie. Reggie grinned and swung his stick in preparation.

'Reg, did you happen to be around yesterday arvo? Keeping your eyes open?'

The stick struck the can firmly but imparted a twist and it flew off into the bush beside the road. Reggie stopped and stared after it helplessly. Huck moved off the road, stepped through the grass and scrub and found a can. Not the same one, but a can. He held it up and Reggie swung his stick.

'Blue car, Reg,' Huck said. 'Jap job. Say, a Toyota. Dusty but pretty new.'

Reggie looked at the can. Huck set it on the dirt beside the bitumen. Reggie hit it and the can flew through the air, landed and rolled.

'LPP three eight four,' Reggie said.

Two hours and several phone calls later Huck knew that the blue Toyota was registered in the name of a Bega car hire company and had been stolen the day before. Huck's contacts in the New South Wales police force were many and varied and he was able to get the message through that, if the car was located, a certain person in Canberra should be contacted. A long shot at best, more likely a dead end, but Huck was not discouraged. The stealing of hire cars to perform covert operations was not usual. In fact, in Huck's experience, it was unique to a particular man. A man whose credentials included exceptional marksmanship with a rifle. The next step was to start pushing buttons, applying pressure, calling in favours that would extract information from the Department of Immigration. He needed to know whether Lewis 'Kiwi' Draper, aka Allan Drake, aka Leonard Allan Driscoll, born Auckland, New Zealand, 31/2/59, was in Australia.

As he thumbed through his contact book, a battered, dog-eared item, much crossed-out and written over, Huck meditated on his decision to retire from the FSA to the quiet of the south coast. It had seemed like a good idea at the time and he supposed it still was. He had caught up on a lot of lost sleep and pulled in a lot of fish, but sometimes he missed the old excitement. And here he was, phone in hand, trying to track Kiwi Draper, just like the old days. And, truth to tell, he'd have preferred to go fishing. But there was Barry May to think of, and Crawley, and he didn't particularly like being shot at, even as a warning. Huck filled his pipe, put matches on the table, mixed himself a light scotch and water and made the first call.

Crawley had kept away from the archives since coming to Canberra. He didn't like the look of the place in which they were housed. It was all carpeted and beige like a showroom for some discreet consumer product. He preferred the old, musty cavern in Melbourne that smelled of rats and dust, although he hadn't ventured into the Melbourne archives for some years either, disliking the creeping modernisation. Having to make an appointment to see Rupert Dacre annoyed him. An archive, in his opinion, should be somewhere you could come and go, maybe with someone to frisk you on the way out to make sure you weren't pinching the manilla folders. Not for the first time, Crawley felt that the pace and direction of change in his chosen profession were getting too much for him.

He arrived deliberately early for his appointment and tried to engage the secretary in casual conversation about her job. She went almost catatonic with fear at the sight of him—blue jaws, rumpled hair, tieless and with a button missing from his shirt. She focused on the gap in his shirt; dark, thick hair threatened to burst through. A buzz from her intercom released her from purgatory.

'Dr Dacre will see you now, Mr Crawley.'

'Makes it sound as if I'm here for my haemorrhoids.'

The secretary smiled uncertainly, got up from her desk and opened a door behind her. Crawley didn't like men who liked closed offices; he also didn't like having doors opened for him, but he managed a smile and nod for the frightened young woman. He strolled into the office prepared to dislike Dr Rupert Dacre, who was seated behind his desk riffling through a stack of fax sheets. Dacre stood up and held out his hand.

'Mr Crawley, Rupert Dacre. Good to meet you at last. Please sit down. I would have come to your office but you insisted on coming here so . . .'

Crawley was aware that the archivist was very nervous and he wondered why. He shook hands briefly, dropped into a chair and looked around the room. There was nothing to see, apart from monuments to Dacre's ego. 'Has Hector been in touch with you lately, Rupert? I've just found out what it means to be in the top job—you know bugger all about what's going on.'

Dacre, who in fact had just been handling a fax from Hector Bain in London, smiled politely. 'He keeps in touch. Just in a routine way. Now what can I . . .'

Superior bastard, Crawley thought. *And a born liar. How did we ever get a prick like this on the strength?* Abruptly, he decided not to have any dealings with Dacre. He smelled like one of Hector Bain's boys, all aftershave, bath salts and ambition. He stood up and enjoyed the look of alarm on Dacre's smooth face. 'I want something done,' he said.

'Yes, yes, of course.'

And a wimp to boot. 'I need some research done and I understand some of the files I want to get into are blocked. You'd be the man to unblock them, right?'

'Certainly.'

Crawley took a piece of paper from his shirt pocket, unfolded it and threw it onto Dacre's desk. 'Those are the names and I don't want to keep running up against bloody brick walls every time I try to turn a corner. I want a complete clearance, wherever the trail may lead. Okay?'

'That's a complicated request.'

'I'm sure you can handle it. What's your doctorate in? What field?'

'Communications.'

'There you go. Get on it as soon as you've finished with your faxes.'

Dacre stood, feeling at a disadvantage with Crawley towering over him. 'As you wish. And I take it the clearance is to your terminal, Mr Crawley?'

'Christ, no,' Crawley said. 'I can barely tap out the quick brown fox fucked the lazy dog. Clear it to Boris Stein.'

'We have a problem,' Rupert Dacre said.

Derek Ramsay shook his head. 'I can't see it. What possible difference does it make who relays the information to Crawley?'

'Stein is not reliable. If Crawley becomes suspicious and questions him about anything he will certainly crack. I must say I found Crawley rather a surprise packet. I hadn't expected quite the . . . directness I encountered.'

'Scared you, did he?'

'I wouldn't say that, but he is formidable and will need subtle handling. Stein is certainly not the man to do it.'

Ramsay settled back, prepared to enjoy himself. The

club lounge was busy and he had waved to several acquaintances, drunk a whisky and was feeling expansive. There was too little for intelligence men to exercise their wits on these days in his opinion, and this particular intrigue had a piquancy that was very much to his taste. Not that it wasn't very serious at bottom, it certainly was, but there could be no harm in enjoying the processes. 'I hope you have a solution to your perceived problem, Rupert.'

'I believe it's *our* problem and I have a partial solution only. Some action from you will be required.'

Ramsay's response was to frown and signal languidly to the waiter.

'My secretary is a perceptive young woman of a somewhat nervous disposition,' Dacre said. 'She was rather upset by Crawley and his manner. After he had left she confided certain things to me.'

Ramsay ordered refills. 'I've seen her—a little mousy, but no doubt rousable. Rogering her, are you, you sly dog?'

'If I were I wouldn't tell you. She informs me that Carol Mainwaring, Hector's secretary, is having an affair with Crawley.'

Ramsay raised an eyebrow and Dacre went on. 'Not willingly. He apparently suggested that her job prospects would be dim if she was not compliant.'

Ramsay was unsurprised, having employed this device himself on several occasions. 'So what? Are you suggesting that she bring a sexual harassment case against Crawley? Can't see the point of that.'

'Of course not. Mainwaring is already being useful to us, as you know, keeping tabs on Crawley, serving Hector's interests really.'

Ramsay nodded.

'She is also a highly trained, highly competent computer operator with an excellent knowledge of the systems in use in the intelligence grids. She is the perfect person to serve as our conduit to Crawley.'

'Rupert, I'm impressed. You really are picking up your game. I think you might be right. Crawley has been known to think with his privates in the past. And Mainwaring is definitely one of our assets. I wonder why she didn't tell you about her new closeness to the acting director?'

Dacre was aware of the low regard in which he was held by Carol Mainwaring but he said nothing about this to Ramsay. 'I would be speculating. Perhaps she planned to use it for her own ends, or Hector's. In any case, the information is in our hands now and we would be wise to . . .'

'Yes, yes. But Rupert, what do you want from me?'

'Someone has to get Boris Stein out of the way.'

~ 9 ~

Ruth May sat in the small room that had bars on the windows and a rubber seal around the locked door. An air-conditioner kept the space at a constant temperature, which was neither warm nor cool. After two days she was still struggling against the fact of her captors being the arbiters of the hours for feeding, washing, abluting and exercising, almost the deciders of day and night. She had been given a velour tracksuit and sneakers and she wore them with pleasure, never having owned such things. A pile of back copies of *Reader's Digest* had appeared in her cell and she was devouring them hungrily. She had never opened the magazine before, although she had seen it on newsstands and in medical waiting rooms, and she found it fascinating. Initially compliant, she was starting to be rude and provocative to her guards, seizing the opportunity to abandon good manners.

Being chloroformed had not been pleasant, but she had not otherwise been ill-treated. The food was plain but acceptable, and as she did not smoke and rarely drank she felt no deprivation of essential comforts. Her living space was clean. The two men who attended to her were polite and, so far, unflappable. They were also incommunicative and ignored her requests for information. Questioned as to where she was, why she was being held prisoner and how long her imprisonment would last brought no response. The only information she was given came from the larger and older of the two guards. He was an impressive figure in casual clothes, resembling a business executive on holiday. He walked with a pronounced limp on the left side.

'Do as you're told,' he had said, 'and you'll come to no harm. You have my word on that.'

'And what if I don't do as I'm told?' Ruth had asked.

'You're not stupid, Miss May, so please don't behave as if you are.'

Ruth exercised in a high-walled courtyard, doing callisthenics barely remembered from her schooldays, and walking the perimeter. She had read numerous books about the experience of imprisonment, from Dumas to Dick Francis and, as an insomniac, had watched many episodes of an old British TV series called 'Prisoner'. For a time she enjoyed putting some of the precepts she had learned into practice. As far as she could tell she had not been transported far. The weather and temperature by day and night were much the same as they had been in Canberra. The wall was too high to see over and care had been taken to remove anything climbable, but she could see trees in the near distance and hear birds rather than road noise. She was undoubtedly in the country. A few planes flew high overhead but she had never paid air traffic any attention and could draw no conclusions from their direction or elevation. The house was possibly large, but the courtyard enclosed only a small two-storey back section and gave her no accurate perspective of the whole.

By the beginning of the third day boredom had set in and she had become irritable and uncooperative. In the courtyard she prised up a stone, threw it at her guard, missed and broke a window. The senior attendant ushered her back from the exercise session and followed her into the cell.

'You are being foolish,' he said.

'I'm frightened.'

'I've told you . . .'

'You've told me fucking nothing!'

'There's no need to be abusive.'

'This is all a game to you, isn't it?'

The attendant smiled urbanely. 'You might put it like that, if it makes you feel any better.'

'What will make me feel better is to get out of here.'

'I'm sorry.'

'Please tell me why this is happening. I'm afraid I'll go mad.'

'I thought you were holding up pretty well, if I may say so.'

'Jesus! You've done this before, haven't you?'

The man appeared to consider carefully before replying. He stroked an incipient jowl, drawing the slackening skin tighter. 'Oh, yes.'

'Your good manners are giving me the shits.'

'I'm disappointed in you, Miss May. Good day.'

Ruth slumped on the bed and stared at the locked, sealed door. She picked up a copy of the *Reader's Digest* and hurled it at the wall. She closed her eyes, lay back and tried to find some source of comfort. An image of Crawley came into her mind—swarthy, untidy, pugnacious, more than a match for her well-groomed ageing captor. For a moment she allowed herself to hope and then a dark thought invaded her consciousness: *It might have been him that put me in here!*

Allan Drake had entered Australia from Singapore two weeks previously, Huck learned. There were no outstanding warrants against him; his Interpol file was marked 'inactive' and he was not subject to surveillance by Australian police or any branch of the intelligence services. The prospects for tracking his movements within the country were poor but Huck played a hunch and got lucky. A Leonard Driscoll had crossed Bass Strait to Tasmania three days before the death of Laura Hopkins. It was not a wildly uncommon name, but Huck was confident that it was his man. Here the trail ended except for the information that Drake/ Driscoll/Draper had not left Australia. Illiberal by nature, Huck lamented that Australia, unlike other countries, allowed foreigners to move around freely. Without giving a name Kiwi Draper could have travelled by train or bus to anywhere, such as the south coast or Canberra.

Getting hold of a high-powered, semi-automatic rifle was tougher than it used to be, but still well within Draper's capabilities. Huck could smell his spoor on this path of violence and disruption. *What's scary about Kiwi*, he thought, *is that he's not a sicko—he can kill, but he doesn't have to.* It was time to inform Crawley of the new development. He telephoned to Canberra but was told that the acting director was unavailable. Huck left his number and an urgent request for Crawley to ring. He felt frustrated. He would have liked to go after Draper but he didn't have the resources. Huck whistled for Toby and set off for a long walk through the dunes and along the beach. He knew that he'd end up on the rocky shelf where Barry May's hat and the fishing gear alleged to be his had been found. The body had come ashore further up the coast. Perhaps he'd even walk that far. He missed Barry. Over his shoulder he slung a canvas bag. Inside the bag was an old but carefully tended Erma

71

MP40 machine pistol. Huck was suspicious of Germans in general, but he had to admit they made good guns.

Boris Stein, a bachelor, lived in Queanbeyan in a quiet street. His weatherboard house, of which he was the only occupant, was large, but over the years his computer equipment had expanded to fill it. He was a man of regular, somewhat old-fashioned habits. He had his newspapers and a 600 ml carton of milk delivered daily and he took these items in from his front doorstep at 7 a.m. precisely. Ten minutes later he would have perused the headlines and be pouring fresh milk on his muesli. The milk left over from the day before he gave to his cat, Toshiba.

Boris performed his rituals, sneered at the political news, turned to the business pages and spooned in his muesli. When the bowl was empty he crossed to the sink and ran water into it. A wave of nausea hit him but he couldn't vomit. He clung on to the edge of the sink as his legs wobbled under him. He retched and nothing happened. His chest burned and his head began to throb violently. He flailed, knocked the milk carton from the table, fell in a heap on the cold linoleum and curled up into a ball, whimpering as pain seized him in the guts and ran through him like an electric current. Then the cramps gripped him—in the stomach and leg muscles. He screamed and writhed on the floor. The cat leaped to the top of the refrigerator and gazed down on the stricken man.

A stream of Polish, German and gibberish poured from Boris as he crawled across the floor, stopping when the pain cut his breath. Sweat broke out on his forehead and ran down into his eyes. He moaned and resumed crawling, drawing his legs up and thrusting back, making slow progress. He gained the living room and began inching across the threadbare carpet towards the telephone sitting on a low table. Twice he stopped and waited for waves of pain and icy cramps to subside. He became entangled in an extension cord and almost fainted with the effort of freeing himself.

Boris's father had survived Auschwitz. He had told his son about the freezing cattle trucks, the back-breaking work, the starvation and humiliation. Boris had grown up in the soft embrace of Australian suburbia and often wondered if he could have displayed his father's toughness. Through the blasts of pain he was dimly aware of a challenge that was being extended to him. *You can die here on this ratty carpet,* he thought, *or you can get to that fucking phone and live.* The carpet smelled of cat piss, which enraged him. He lunged forward, gripped the leg of the table and shook the telephone off. It fell and bounced out of his reach. Boris's head hit the floor and he shut his eyes. The cat mewed and jumped down from the refrigerator. It lapped at the spilt milk on the kitchen floor.

Boris opened his eyes and blinked as the sweat stung them. The telephone was a metre away, the longest distance he had ever contemplated travelling; an impossible gulf. He had no feeling in his feet and the cold was creeping up his legs. He gave a terrified twitch, got a purchase somehow and flopped forward. He grabbed the phone and stabbed at it, getting a dial tone, tapping out the number.

'An ambulance,' he gasped. 'Vivian Street, Queanbeyan, number twenty-six. Hurry please!'

It was almost thirty minutes before the ambulance

arrived. The paramedics found Boris unconscious on the floor. His colour was bad and his pulse was weak. They injected adrenalin and loaded him onto the stretcher. One of them spotted the cat, stretched out stiffly on the kitchen floor, its tongue lying in a pool of spilt milk. While Boris was being inserted into the ambulance he called the police.

~ 10 ~

After his meeting with Rupert Dacre, Crawley had felt the need to breathe non-official air. He had left the building and gone to the Manuka squash centre where he'd engaged in several hard games against younger, fitter players. He stopped when he suspected a slight groin strain, cursing age, old injuries, squash racquets and all young men. A swim and a sauna improved his physical condition and his mood. He decided against going back to the office. *Let 'em worry,* he thought. He couldn't expect Boris to have anything for him until the morning at the earliest. Ruth May's disappearance troubled him greatly, but there was nothing he could do about it. It was part of a broader pattern and he was trying to find a way into that, with Huck's help and Boris's.

One of Crawley's strengths as an intelligence field agent was his objectivity. He didn't agonise over what couldn't be changed, still less did he waste energy on appearing to be busy. To an extent, he thought and acted according to sporting metaphors and precepts— he would give 110 per cent when it was required, and coast when there was nothing to be gained by trying. Which is why he stopped on the way home to buy wine and avocados and feta cheese and the salty olives that Mandy loved. 'The cure for one woman is another,' a highly experienced male friend had told him and Crawley had found it to be true, with a quirk—over time, his wife had cured him of numerous other women.

He entered the house, carrying the groceries and whistling his flat, energetic version of 'The Road to Mandalay'—an old, bad joke.

'Mandy.'

The house was quiet, empty. He found the note on the kitchen bench:

Ray

Crisis in Melbourne. Have flown there for a couple of days. Will ring when can. Take care.

love

    M.

Morosely, Crawley opened one of the bottles of wine and poured a full glass which he tossed straight down. He poured another and looked at his purchases. The avocados spilled out onto the formica top and he realised that he didn't know what to do with them. Mandy prepared some kind of sharp-tasting dressing, but he didn't know the ingredients. He flicked through the pile of mail Mandy had left in the kitchen. It was mostly bills but there was a letter from Vanessa, his daughter, now living in a lesbian relationship in Montana and breeding quarter-horses. Crawley couldn't bring himself to open it.

He prowled through the house, drinking and growing more disgruntled as he went. He eyed the expensive furniture, most of it seldom used. He stared out through the French windows at the pool he hadn't swum in for months. He paid a Vietnamese man who had been a bank manager in Saigon to cut the grass; a Uruguayan woman cleaned the house once a week; when he remembered he put plastic and glass bottles in a box beside the stacked newspapers for the recycling service to take away.

'Jesus,' he said. 'What a way to live.'

Back in the kitchen he watched the news on television and made rough sandwiches from the avocado, cheese and olives. He opened the second bottle of wine. The food tasted lousy. An image of Ruth May came into his head as he clicked off the TV—the young Mandy, smooth and new, with a narrow waist and a thick mane of hair . . . The phone rang and Crawley grabbed for it.

'Mandy?'

'This is Huck, Creepy. You sound shithouse. What's the matter with you?'

'Nothing. If you're hoping to hear about those cards, forget it. Tomorrow at the earliest.'

'This is something else,' Huck said.

Huck's surmises and information about Kiwi Draper acted as a tonic for Crawley. His instincts for the aroma of deception, bluff and double-dealing were activated and he began to feel that things were taking shape. He told Huck he'd institute a search for Draper and put a tail on him if he were found.

'I'd like to talk to him,' Huck said.

'You've got no status.'

'I've got a fucking *interest*!'

Crawley acknowledged that and promised to keep Huck informed. He told him about the degree of progress with the Holorith cards. 'I've seen the archivist and he's agreed to give me an open go at the files. Boris'll be hopping into it tomorrow. It has to be all about something in the records. You know what occurs to me?'

'What?'

'Your mate May might have been blackmailing someone and they caught up with him.'

'Bullshit. Barry was as straight a bloke as you'd ever hope to see.'

'Did you ever meet John Frederick?'

'No.'

'Neither did I, but people who did tell me they'd have trusted him with their wife, daughter, keycard, PIN number, whatever.'

'You're on the wrong track. Look, Creepy, I'd like to be in on this. I know Kiwi Draper by sight and I could . . .'

'We'll see,' Crawley said. 'I'll be in touch.'

He hung up through Huck's protest and moved across to one of the overflowing bookshelves that were the despair of Maria, the house-cleaner. She tried to keep the books tidy in their shelves and well dusted, but both Crawley and Mandy were careless with books, losing the jackets, turning down the pages, throwing them into the shelves any old how. It took Crawley several minutes to find the small, slim volume self-published in 1983 by Wilfred Sparks. Entitled *Patriotism—Prudent and Patient*, the book was the memoirs of the FSA director immediately preceding Toby Campion. Crawley had once tried to read it and given up, unable to cope with the unusual combination of hilarity and tedium it had generated. He had declared it one of the worst books ever published. He had taken it out once for a laugh since arriving in Canberra and shoved it back, spine first, where it had become obscured by paperbacks.

He took it to a chair and turned the pages, taking care not to read the pompous, inflated prose, lest it send him off into a paroxysm of laughter or rage. In particular he avoided the photographs which inevitably showed tubby little Wilfred in the company of the likes of Eisenhower, Churchill and Menzies. Crawley located the half-remembered passage and read:

It is a regrettable fact that the implementation of

*the Freedom of Information Act coincided with
the substantive phase of the changeover from
manual and mechanical to fully computerised
record-keeping. Extra burdens were placed on the
archival system with which it was in no way
equipped to cope. I fear that requests for release
of information were sometimes confused with
demands for rapid computerisation of the same
data and some materials were lost. Perhaps more
seriously, top secret files may have been exposed
to the eyes of those not of a sufficiently high
security-cleared status to legitimately see them.*

*Future holders of my post may suffer as a result
of the devastating pressures which were brought
to bear on loyal servants of the crown in those
days. Goals were lost sight of and principles
abandoned in a desperate search for the fleeting
and fickle imprimatur of popularity, cunningly
masked as 'accountability'. I believe I have
nothing to reproach myself with.*

*I welcomed the move to electronic storage and
processing in the interests of efficiency and
deplored the kowtowing to the fashionable
'liberal' notion of freedom of information. As we
in the intelligence services knew only too well,
information was often paid for in spilled
blood . . .*

Dopey old turd, Crawley thought, *the nearest you
ever got to spilled blood was a paper cut*. Nevertheless,
the passage was interesting. It could be interpreted as
supporting the blackmail theory that placed Barry May
(and Laura Hopkins, for that matter) as perpetrators,
ultimately caught up with and eliminated by their

victims. Or hirelings thereof. Neat, if backed up in some way by the information that would come soon to Boris. But what if there was no support for the theory in the flow-on from the Holorith cards? And what of the high-velocity warning to Huck and the disappearance of Ruth May?

Crawley slammed *Patriotism—Prudent and Patient* shut and returned it to the shelves. Wilfred Sparks had sent the book to every serving FSA officer and blitzed the media with complimentary copies. It had never received a review in the mainstream press. Crawley remembered the derision it had occasioned in the Melbourne office. FSA men reading out paragraphs while flapping their wrists and aping Sparks's mannerisms—the waggled cigarette holder, the much-adjusted bow tie, the aggressive, cocky, small man's strut.

Crawley, at that time assigned to the 'garbage collectors', a counter-terrorist, counter-subversion unit with a broad brief and considerable executive authority, had seen very little of Director Sparks. Like others, he had mocked him as a fossil, a relic of an earlier, simpler time. He corked the second bottle of wine and brewed a pot of coffee. He added a slug of brandy to his full cup and toasted the memory of the little man in the bow tie.

'You had a point, Wilf,' he said. 'Future holders of your post may suffer.'

Ruth May was speculating about the reasons for her captivity. Her own life had contained nothing that could have led to it. It was almost ironic: she had struggled to free herself from her father's benign influence and here she was, a prisoner of *his* enemies.

Or, she reminded herself, *of his friends.* But she knew nothing about her father's work, was privy to no secrets. Why then, lock her up? Obviously to provoke a reaction in someone. Who? There her analysis ran out. The only person she could think of was Crawley. The passivity of her position infuriated her. The bland diet provided by the *Reader's Digest* began to make her acutely aware of her powerlessness. She refused to accept it. She determined to provoke some reactions of her own.

On a visit to the bathroom, escorted by the younger minder, she asked for hair shampoo and a comb and was given her complete make-up purse, minus the scissors and tweezers. She showered, washed her hair, spent some time in front of the mirror, restoring her face, arranging her hair and contriving the sort of femininity of appearance she despised. When the attendant opened the door he was surprised to see her wrapped in a towel and carrying her tracksuit.

'I want to put my dress on,' she said. 'I'm sick of wearing this thing.'

'You'll be cold.'

'Get me a shirt or something then. You must have some decent shirts. Got a silk one?'

Back in the cell she slipped into the dress and smoothed out its wrinkles. The high-heeled shoes would have helped but they were missing, no doubt viewed as possible weapons. The door opened and the guard handed her a white silk shirt. Ruth took it, shrugged it on and knotted it around the waist. 'Don't go,' she said.

'You're wasting your time.'

'I want something to draw with.'

'What?'

'I'm going crazy in here, reading this crap and staring at the wall. Get me a sketch pad and a soft pencil to help me pass the time. It's not much to ask.'

A shake of the head. 'No pencil. No way.'

'Okay, okay, I understand. I could stab you with it. A crayon then, A big fat crayon. Please!'

His eyes were on her. She could feel them. It was a good feeling—empowering. At last she was making an impact and was close to getting her own way on something. Very close.

'I'll see.' The door closed and the seal firmed around it. Ruth sat down on the bed and felt the fluffed out shape of her hair. The reappearance of the make-up purse was a surprise. It had been a present from someone and she had scarcely used it before the night she stuffed it into the bag she took to the Lake Royal. She kept her nails short but had been about ready to cut them before she got the news of her father's death. Such trivial things had dropped out of her consciousness and now her nails had grown quite long. She shaped them with an emery board (the nail file had also been removed) and began to paint them carefully, something she had not done since her early teens. *Before I became a blue stocking*, she thought.

As she worked she thought back over her life to those times of hormonal disturbance—the crushes on the older girls at school, the tentative gropings with boys after inter-school dances; the first, alcohol-driven act of intercourse. She had always had the ability to attract men, she knew that. But usually the wrong sorts of men. And she could repel them, too, by being too sharp for them, too quick, too critical. She smoothed the thick paint onto her right thumbnail and spread it, surprised at how easily the skill came back. She thought about the guard. How old? Thirty at most. A New Zealander to judge by the accent. Not bad looking but with a lot of anger pent up inside. A dangerous man. Like Crawley. *God damn it, why do I keep thinking about that man?* Back to the New Zealander. Gay? Unlikely, he was interested; but then I was wearing his shirt. It's hard to tell with men these days.

'What's your name?' she asked when the guard opened the door.

'Silly question. Here, will these do?'

Ruth looked at the big, spiral-bound sketchbook and the packet of thick crayons. 'Terrific, thanks.'

'Tell you what, call me Dee. It's one of my initials, but it'll do for a name. What are you going to draw?'

'I may surprise you.'

Dee was standing with his back to the door. He was balanced and alert, putting out more energy than before. 'You've already surprised me. I thought you were one of those women's lib types, all serious like. No laughs.'

I'm getting to him, Ruth thought. She shook her head and the shampooed hair flew. 'Not me. Where are you from, Dee, Auckland?'

The good-natured expression disappeared from the lean face. He tightened up, physically and emotionally. 'Listen to me. Don't try to find out things about us. It won't do you any good. It might do you some harm. Didn't the other bloke tell you that?'

'He told me to do as I was told and I'd be all right.'

'That's right.'

'I don't believe him.'

'You should. I've got to go. I'll bring you something to eat in a couple of hours. Will you have a drawing to show us by then?'

'Maybe.'

He was looking down the front of her dress. He cleared his throat, muttered something and went out. Ruth continued painting her nails. They were nice nails, strong and well shaped. She thought that they could probably do a lot of damage to the tight skin on that hard-boned face.

~ 11 ~

Crawley spent the first part of the morning putting the wheels in motion to locate Kiwi Draper. The procedures were familiar and somehow comforting. He felt he was doing something constructive at last. He dealt with the routine tasks that took up much of the director's time and asked Carol Mainwaring to give any call from Boris Stein top priority. It was almost midday when she came into his office. Crawley looked up from the report he was annotating. The secretary wore a black silk blouse with shoulder pads and loose sleeves and a straight white skirt. Her dark hair was drawn back severely and her heavily made-up eyes were large and dramatic in her thin face.

'Yes, Carol?'

'Mr Stein was taken to Queanbeyan hospital early this morning.'

'What's the matter with him? An accident?'

'No. He seems to be suffering from food poisoning. He's very ill.'

'Bugger it,' Crawley said. 'I was counting on him to do something for me. Must be serious if he's in hospital. Did they say how long he'd be there?'

Carol Mainwaring shrugged. The movement lifted her small firm bosom and Crawley experienced a twinge of lust. 'The hospital says he was on the critical list at first. They don't fear for his life now, but it must be pretty bad.'

'Poor old Boris,' Crawley said. 'I thought all he ever ate was lentils. Must've let 'em soak too long or something. I'll have to look in on him. Leaves me with a big problem though.'

'Can I help?'

Crawley pushed his chair back and looked at her, trying to steer his way mentally past the automatic sexual appraisal. One of Mandy's constant themes was the male sexual response from the patriarchal power base. He had heard it expounded so often he had come to understand it. Well, here was the classic situation. He wanted to fuck her but would he let her do an important job? A job that might help advance her career. Or would he go and see Boris, sick and all as he was, and get a recommendation from him—operate the boy's network, as Mandy called it?

'How good are you with computers?'

'Very good.'

Crawley made his decision. 'I had a discussion with Dr Dacre yesterday about getting clearance on certain files and associated . . . sensitive information. What's your clearance level?'

'A2, not topmost but very high.'

'Shit, I don't even know what I'm talking about. Would you be able to transfer the clearance from Stein's terminal to yours, if I give you the authority?'

Carol Mainwaring smiled. 'Of course. All I have to do is go back to my terminal and send a message to Dr Dacre's terminal via yours. You respond with an affirmative to the prompt.'

Crawley sighed and loosened his tie. He slipped the knot down and undid the top shirt button. 'Do it, Carol. Please do it. I'll sit here and look at the bloody thing. You come in and tell me what to do.'

She was back within ten minutes, leaning over his shoulder and telling him what keys to hit. He smelled her perfume and the clean body odours, uncontaminated by tobacco or alcohol or cooking. It had been a long time since he'd experienced anything so pure and sexually lethal.

'That should do it,' Carol said. 'You'll have to give me some idea of what the information will be about. I mean, will I need to work in graphics, mathematical parameters . . .?'

Crawley groaned. 'You're giving me a headache, Carol. Why don't we go out and have some lunch. I'll tell you all . . . no, as much as I can, about it over a bit of fish and salad and a glass of wine. You do drink wine, don't you?'

'Dry white,' Carol said.

'Me, too. Also rough red. I've never been much of a luncher in Canberra, where's good?'

Carol had to struggle to prevent triumph showing on her face. She looked away from Crawley's hot eyes and pretended to think. 'There's a funny little place in Forrest. I don't know how they got a licence and I don't know how they keep going. You don't have to book. It's terribly quiet, but the food's great and it's not too dear. I mean, it's not silly.'

'Sounds good,' Crawley said. 'You mop up your desk and I'll do the same. Ten minutes, okay?'

Carol turned and walked away from Crawley, careful not to exaggerate a single movement. As she reached her desk she felt her heart thump in her narrow chest and heat surge into her face. *He's hooked*, she thought, *well and truly*. She tidied her desk and put through a quick call to Dr Rupert Dacre.

Huck's walk failed to soothe him. A wind had got up, stirring the sand and blowing it into his face. Toby was uncharacteristically playful, running off to chase windblown objects, barking at seagulls and generally behaving like an idiot. Huck stood on the rocky shelf where Barry May's things had been found and looked out to sea. It wasn't even a good fishing spot and a child could see how dangerous it could be if a swell was running, not that there'd been one on the day Barry had gone. Huck kicked savagely at a piece of kelp, which skittered away. Toby chased it, brought it back, but Huck wasn't in the mood for games. Freak wave my arse, he thought.

A sound behind him made him spin and crouch. His hand flew into the canvas bag, gripped the MP40, withdrew and levelled it in a practised motion.

'Shit, Mr Huck, don't do that, mate. It's only me.'

Reggie Carmichael stood four metres away, slowly raising his hands. Huck returned the gun to its bag. 'Shouldn't sneak up on a man like that, Reg,' he said.

'Didn't sneak up, not me. Bloody wind and that. Even Toby didn't hear me.'

Huck was in no mood for company. 'You want something, Reg?'

The dog reacted to his master's tone and growled but Carmichael stood his ground and allowed himself to be sniffed at. 'You know me, Toby. You know me all right, boy. Nothing, Mr Huck. Just wanted to know if LPP three eight four was any use. Funny thing, I tell people stuff but they never tell me if it was what they wanted, like. Sorry, Mr Huck.'

Huck had two muesli bars in the bag as well as the gun. Reggie flinched as Huck dug into it but smiled when he saw the sweet. 'Sorry, Reg,' Huck said. 'Nerves are shot. Want one of these?'

Reg accepted the bar and peeled away the cellophane wrapping. Huck unwrapped the other and gave half to Toby. Reg munched contentedly, mumbling with his hard gums and few remaining teeth. He gazed out at the breakers. 'Mr May was your mate, wasn't he?'

'Yeah, he was.'

'I seen him with that bloke in the blue car, LPP, three eight four. Didn't like that bloke.'

Huck stopped chewing. 'Who didn't like him? You or Barry?'

'Me 'n him both, I reckon. Looked like a stoush comin' on, then the other bloke stepped in.'

The wind whipped away Carmichael's words and Huck had to move closer to him to hear. He could smell neglect and solitariness on him, familiar smells, intensified by Reg's feeble-mindedness. Huck spoke gently. 'Where was this, Reg?'

'Up in the town, like. Near the pub. Mr May was buying some grog.'

Huck knew that his friend bought his abstemious ration, most of which Huck usually drank, on Thursday afternoon. Carmichael was talking about the day Barry May died. 'What happened?'

'Aw, I dunno. They talked and then your mate got into this white car with the other bloke, not the one with the blue car.'

'Did you get the number of the white car?'

'Nup. I was too far away, but I seen it pretty good. Had fishing gear on the top, you know, what d'they call it up there . . .?'

'Roof rack.'

Carmichael didn't react to the word but Huck had known him to enquire about words and phrases before and show no interest in the answer. 'Coupla rods up there.'

'What did he look like?'

'Who, Mr Huck?'

'The driver of the blue car.'

Carmichael was sucking on the bar now, making it last. He dribbled down his chin and onto his jacket. 'Didn't see him. He was inside his car. Your mate was sorta leaning on it.'

'You saw the driver of the white car though?'

'Yeah.'

'Well?'

'What?'

Huck fought to control the exasperation. 'What did *he* look like?'

'Aw, big bloke, Mr Huck. About your size I reckon, but he was . . .'

'Go on, Reg.'

Carmichael was not completely witless and he had long ago learned to avoid offending people. His sense of what might give offence, however, was far from perfect. He grinned, pulled off his knitted cap, and ran his hand over his grizzled untidy hair. 'Hadda lotta hair, Mr Huck. Thick hair, all white, same colour as the car. Not an old bloke, but he had all this white hair, real thick it was, too . . .'

'Okay, okay. Anything else about him?'

Carmichael scratched his bristly chin, discovered the dried saliva and picked at it. 'No, 'cept for a gammy leg.' He whacked his right thigh heavily. 'This one.'

Jesus Christ, that sounds like Gerard Thornton, Huck thought. *Bugger Crawley. I'm going to Canberra!*

Ruth May worked hard at the sketch. Drawing was a skill that had come easily to her back in her schooldays, but she had never 'done anything with it'. Now, she found great enjoyment in trying to get the likeness. She drew the outline with quick, fluid strokes and began to shade in the detail. The bald head wasn't a great problem. But the nose, how had that been? Crooked, surely, probably broken at some time. The chin, full and rounded; not quite a double chin, but a suggestion of it. She got close on the first attempt but wasn't satisfied. She tore out the leaf, screwed it up and began again. After all, she had all the time in the world.

The second effort was a failure—the eyes were wrong, all wrong. They had to be smaller and more widely spaced. Another crumpled sheet hit the floor. The next shot felt better from the beginning. She was confident now, having smoothed out the rough spots. The face was emerging convincingly under her crayon. This was it! She added the prominent adam's apple and suggested the ruddy, roughened complexion. She had only the ears to go and they eluded her for a time— prominent, but not wingnuts. *Where had she got that expression from?* She remembered—from her father; his description of one of her primary school boyfriends. She smiled at the recollection and finished the drawing, supplying the suggestion of the thick neck in the open shirt, the breadth of chest beneath.

She sat back and examined the result critically. This was him, definitely. She tore another sheet from the pad and carefully removed the paper caught in the spiral binding. This she reduced to a tiny ball and swallowed. The spare blank sheet she placed under the mattress. She broke an inch from the crayon and hid it inside the pillowcase. She rubbed the crayon vigorously on one of the soiled sheets to shape it to a point. She poured water from the plastic jug into the plastic mug, sipped it and waited.

When the door opened she had the sketch lying face-down on the bed. Dee entered the room cautiously and put the tray on the floor just inside the door. Ruth examined him closely. He'd combed his hair, maybe even freshened up his shave. He looked confident, self-satisfied. Again his eyes went over her, taking in the mane of hair, the bare throat, the big eyes.

'Well,' he said, 'what've you got to show me?'

Ruth placed her hand over the sheet. 'What're you expecting?'

'Oh, I don't know. I'll take what I get.'

Arrogant shit. She remembered the Carly Simon song:

You're so vain

I bet you think this song is about you . . .

'Not much chance of landscape. I can't see a bloody thing from here or from the courtyard.'

Dee shrugged. 'So I guess you just have to use your imagination.'

'Right. I thought I might try a picture of your dick, but I've never seen it.'

'That could be arranged.'

'Or Mr Smoothie's. Which would be bigger, I wonder?'

Dee frowned. 'I don't think you're in the best position to play cock-teasing games.'

'Go on, you don't mean it.'

Dee reached for the paper; Ruth jumped from the bed and lunged towards the open door but he was far too quick for her. He caught her by the arm and easily flipped her to the floor. 'That was dumb. Now, let's have a look.'

He turned the sheet over and stared at the face of a bald-headed man with a thick neck, heavy shoulders and the battered face of an all-in wrestler. 'Jesus,' he said.

Ruth watched the signs of recognition and alarm play over Dee's regular features. *That's got you worried*, she thought. *What are you going to do about it, you arsehole?*

~ 12 ~

Crawley had never seen the restaurant before but he had strong memories of the motel next door. It was one he had used for a series of assignations during a brief separation from Mandy. A crisis—a shark attack on their surfer son, Simon—had brought them back together. The boy had survived a serious wound and considerable loss of blood without long-term damage, but the shock to Crawley and Mandy had been profound and had led to new, still virtually intact, resolutions of fidelity. As he pulled his BMW into the restaurant's parking lot, Crawley looked at Carol Mainwaring's bony knees, exposed by the riding up of her tight skirt. The skirt was up higher than it needed to be, and then there was the motel . . .

They entered the restaurant, a converted house in the older style of Canberra's middle-class residences, and were shown to a table overlooking a courtyard garden. Beyond that, Crawley could just catch a glimpse of the motel sign. It was unilluminated in the daytime, but he was pretty sure that there would be a vacancy.

'Favourite place of yours, Carol?' Crawley asked as he accepted the wine list.

'Hardly that. I've been here once or twice. Any kind of fish is fine and they've got a greenhouse out the back where they grow the salad stuff.'

'Sounds good. Drink?'

'Some white wine with the meal. If you get the bottle now I'll have a spritzer first.'

Crawley ordered a white burgundy and a split of soda water. When the wine came he mixed Carol

Mainwaring's drink and poured a glass for himself. He ordered oysters and bream with salad.

'I'll have the same.'

They touched glasses. The talk over the meal was inconsequential. Crawley was careful not to interrogate and Carol Mainwaring's contributions mainly concerned the food, life in Canberra (she was from Fremantle, but had worked in London and New York) and routine FSA chat. The restaurant was sufficiently patronised to satisfy the management, but they were able to talk in normal tones without fear of being overheard. *If the bloody table isn't bugged*, Crawley thought.

Carol Mainwaring ordered a chocolate mousse dessert and, from the way she ate it, Crawley concluded that she was either a frustrated actress or chocolate affected her glands. Her eyes appeared to enlarge and her shark-like mouth curved until it resembled something softer, if no less deadly. She pushed her shoulders back and her high, pointed breasts seemed to stab at his eyes. Crawley had no difficulty convincing himself that he was now engaged in a covert operation and would have to play the part he'd been allotted.

'I love chocolate,' Carol Mainwaring licked her thin lips. She wanted to smoke but she knew Crawley's eccentric views. She'd heard him say that smoking was harmless—if done between the ages of fourteen and twenty.

'You do,' Crawley said. 'What else do you like?'

'A lot of things.' She drained the last drops from her glass. Crawley signalled for the bill, tended his credit card and signed the slip. Carol Mainwaring gazed out at the garden while Crawley attended to these details. She looked at the small watch she wore on a narrow black band.

'I'm the boss, remember?' Crawley said. 'You're not late back when you're with me.'

'I suppose not. Still, if you want me to get on with that job . . .'

Crawley stood. 'There's no hurry.'

Carol Mainwaring was a little below average height but she wore high heels and stood very straight. Crawley watched her smooth her skirt over her flat stomach, suck air in and push out her chest. She smiled at him and her dark eyes were like promises of pleasure. His fingers wanted to explore the sharp angles of her face. As they walked from the restaurant he put his hand on the small of her back and felt her tremble. He steered her away from the car, towards the motel and she followed the movement like a well-disciplined ballroom dancer. Her heels tapped on the concrete. She was breathing quickly and shallowly.

Crawley scribbled something on the registration card and handed it back with a fifty dollar note. The key turned easily in the door of unit ten and they stepped out of sunlight into semi-darkness. Crawley put his hands on the hard, narrow buttocks and pulled her towards him. The ferocity of her response took his breath away. Her sharp teeth nipped into his lower lip and her tongue thrust into his mouth. He ran his hands up her back, feeling the bones and gristle on her thin body. She moaned and pushed her pelvis against him, grinding with hard, sharp hips.

She stepped back and unfastened her blouse and skirt in two fluid movements. Crawley pulled off his jacket and shirt, kicked his shoes away and dropped his trousers. She was in her bra and pantyhose now, white and skinny in the dim room, on her knees in front of him. She jerked down his underpants and took his thickening penis into her mouth for a moment. Then her hands came up and she cupped his testicles while she took a condom from inside her bra and rolled it onto his erection. Through his excitement, Crawley was conscious of the expertise. He reached down and unfastened her bra, pulled her to her feet and closed his hands over the tiny breasts. She fell back on the bed and peeled down her pantyhose. Crawley watched her wriggle back and part her legs. Her thighs were long and thin and her pubic hair was a small, dark smudge.

'Come on,' she said. 'I want you. Come on.'

Crawley lowered himself over her as she thrust up. She guided him inside her and wrapped her legs around him, drawing him down and in. He heard her gasp as he entered her. She was tight and for a moment he thought he would hurt her and held back. She snarled and clawed at him. She thrust up, claiming him and he was past resistance or thought, sinking, pounding down, feeling her thin hardness and not caring as he found a rhythm and they plunged into it together, panting and muttering as their flesh smacked together.

Gerard Thornton had risen high in the Bureau of National Assessment, moving smoothly on from overseas operational duties to executive and administrative assignments at home and abroad. Indeed at one time he had been considered a candidate for the job Derek Ramsay now occupied. He had failed to secure it for reasons never made clear to him, and had seen out his service in a sinecure which had somewhat embittered him. He had been gratified when

Ramsay had called on him some weeks back with the offer of what he called 'a consultancy'.

The exercises in Tasmania and on the south coast had been satisfying to Thornton, the old operative, and the twin tasks of confining Ruth May and controlling Lewis Draper had challenged him as an administrator and organiser. But, unexpectedly and annoyingly, it had become necessary to communicate in person with his principal. It offended his highly developed sense of security to do so, but Ruth May had left him no choice.

'Miss May seems to think she has an ally,' Thornton said.

The two men were settled in the living room of Ramsay's Red Hill house. Ramsay's wife, long accustomed to his clandestine meetings and grateful when they at least took place at home, was watching television several rooms away. Thornton had taken precautions: he had worn a scarf and turned the collar of his coat up, although the evening was mild. A soft felt hat had covered his distinctive silver hair. Ramsay had met him at the door and Thornton had not removed his hat or scarf until well inside the house.

Thornton accepted a cognac and refused a cigar. He was proud of his strong white teeth, all his own despite his age and some dangerous physical encounters. Ramsay puffed on a panatella and wondered how much Thornton's smooth silver hair owed to artifice. 'How can that be?' he said.

'Specifically, Graeme Huck.' Thornton let the words out in a short staccato bark.

'Good lord!'

Thornton took the sketch from his pocket, unfolded it and laid it on the coffee table. 'I thought it unwise to send this by fax. The young woman has a talent, wouldn't you say?'

Ramsay stared down at the baleful face. 'She has indeed. That's Huck to the life. How did she come by the drawing materials?'

Thornton shrugged and sipped his drink. 'She asked for them and I saw no harm in it. She was bored, understandably enough, and becoming a trifle fractious. Draper thought she had taken a fancy to him. I think he expected a portrait of himself. He was considerably disappointed.'

'Is he giving you any trouble?'

Thornton shook his head. Light bounced from his shining hair. 'He's greedy, conceited, moody, but competent enough. I don't expect any difficulty from him. But what about this?'

Regaining his urbanity, Ramsay puffed smoke at the drawing. 'It certainly is an unexpected development. And troubling. Not so much in itself, as in the implications.'

'If she can sketch portraits this well she can certainly capture likenesses of Draper and myself. I confess that worries me. It worries me so much that I'm afraid I'm going to have to put a somewhat unprofessional question to you, Derek.'

Ramsay looked at the drawing and said nothing.

'I would like to know what this is all about. Why are you holding Miss May without interrogating her or subjecting her to any pressure?'

'She hasn't volunteered any information? Say, about the storage and processing of intelligence data?'

'No.'

'Good. In a way, I'd be disappointed if she had. Miss May is simply a pawn in this exercise. Removing her was designed to stir things up in certain quarters. To prompt certain questions that would lead to certain answers.'

Thornton sniffed impatiently. 'Clear as mud.'

'It doesn't have to be clear to you, Gerard. It just has to work. There were always going to be casualties in an operation like this. Inevitably so. It was designed to start severely in Tasmania and Coota Coota and become more benign with Miss May. Unhappily, it looks as if the list may have to be expanded. Still, Huck was a very active agent. There may be benefits. Can you manage the May woman on your own for a time?'

'At some cost to her comfort, yes.'

'That's scarcely a consideration any longer. I think Draper had better go down to Coota Coota again.' Ramsay folded the sketch and put it inside a copy of *Australian Golf Digest* lying near the cut glass ashtray on the coffee table.

Thornton drained his glass. 'An accident?'

Ramsay's smile was thin. 'I don't think we can afford any more marine misadventures. No, I think a disappearance. A complete . . . excision. Is Draper up to it?'

'I believe so. And Miss May?'

'Just . . . wait,' Ramsay said. 'Is there anything else?'

Thornton stood. He was tall, in the mid 180-centimetre range, but dipped slightly on one side—the result of a badly fractured and improperly set leg, the legacy of a violent transaction in Thailand many years before. 'Being greedy, Draper may require some additional financial assurances,' he said. 'In respect of the extra work.'

Ramsay waved his cigar. 'Give them. How can it

matter? What about your own requirements? Have you ever killed a woman, Gerard?'

'I have. More than once. You need have no fears on that score. The present arrangements are entirely satisfactory, Derek.'

Ramsay did not stand. The two men did not shake hands. Thornton left the house without further ceremony. Ramsay, in his chair with a few centimetres of cigar remaining and another measure of brandy in his glass, heard the car start up and pull away. *And I'm not concerned about Miss May drawing your picture accurately, Gerard*, he thought. *I'm concerned about Huck's friend, Ray Crawley.*

Huck left Toby with the Coota pharmacist, who was glad to have a guard dog, even though the last break-in at his shop had occurred five years before when a couple of holiday-makers had stolen several packets of Panadol. Huck set some elaborate booby traps around the house, loaded weapons and equipment of various kinds into his van, and set off to drive to Canberra.

Reggie Carmichael was fishing at the wharf and he waved to him as he went past. The simpleton watched as Huck turned right at the bridge, taking the road south towards the Victorian border. He drove for half a kilometre before turning up a dirt track and cutting across some rough ground to pick up the Canberra road again, well out of sight of the wharf and Carmichael. As he drove, Huck slipped cassettes into the dashboard deck—his taste ran mainly to the instrumental music, light classical and movie themes—and thought about Kiwi Draper and Gerard Thornton as a team. The more he considered it, the more likely it seemed. The hair and the limp—it *had* to be Thornton.

Thornton, he knew, was a member of the intelligence service who had 'retired hurt'. Huck himself was in something of the same category, although his retirement had been forced by his refusal to move to the bureaucrats' heaven of Canberra. Thornton had missed a top job and been put out to graze. Why? Huck searched his memory for the scuttlebutt. It wasn't young girls or small boys. What then? He couldn't remember, but Thornton had had an impressive record as a field agent and he was a survivor. Put him together with Kiwi Draper and you really had a team. The train of thought worried Huck, nagged at him like a cold-sensitive tooth, and it wasn't until he passed Cooma that he recognised the true quality of his concern. As a team, Thornton and Draper were uncomfortably close to Crawley and Huck.

~ 13 ~

Crawley and Carol scarcely spoke on the drive back
to the FSA building. Both were shaken by the intensity
of the encounter. Her normally pale face was flushed
and her thin mouth looked puffy and bruised.
Crawley's legs were still shaking; he drove badly,
misjudging distances and failing to take turns cleanly.
The scratches on his back stung and he was pretty sure
there would be blood on his shirt. He stopped at the
entrance and leaned across to open the door. Carol gave
off a musky odour, a combination of wine, perfume
and sex, which forced him to touch her. He put his
hand on her thigh and she stroked it with her long,
bony fingers.

'I've got something to do,' he said huskily. 'I'll be
back later.'

She kept the triumph out of her voice with an effort.
'I'll see if anything's come through on . . . that
matter.'

'Good.'

She collected her bag and left the car. Crawley
watched her narrow hips sway slightly as she went up
the stairs on her high heels. She was composing herself
with each step, straightening her blouse, patting her
hair. *By the time she reaches her desk she'll look as
if she's had a sandwich and a Diet Coke by the lake*,
he thought. He pulled away and headed for
Queanbeyan.

By the time he reached the hospital he had put all
thought of the woman out of his head. He gave his
name, asked to see Boris and was shown to a waiting
room where five or six people sat in various stages of

uneasiness. Hospitals depressed Crawley. His father had died in one and his mother, Sicilian that she was, enjoyed their mordant atmosphere. Now in her mid-sixties and entirely healthy, she actively sought opportunities for brief hospitalisations. Crawley eyed his fellow visitors with suspicion. After ten minutes a young, overweight uniformed police officer entered the waiting room and approached him.

'Mr Cawley?'

'Crawley.'

'Would you come with me, sir?'

'Why?'

The policeman glanced around the room. 'Just a few questions. Be better in private.'

Crawley stood and allowed the policeman to shepherd him out. In the corridor he spun and confronted him. 'What's all this about?'

'I'm afraid I can't . . .'

'What's your name, Senior Constable? Crawley barked.

'Ted, sir, I mean . . . Edward.' The policeman found Crawley's aggressive body language and fierce stare unlike anything he had experienced before. 'That is, Jack . . . Jackson.'

Crawley produced his identity card. 'I don't want to heavy you, son, but I outrank you the way Ali outranked Bugner, do you understand me?'

Senior Constable Edward Jackson didn't understand the reference, not exactly, but he recalled his training and recognised the card. He nodded. 'Yes, sir.'

'Okay. Now take me up to see Mr Stein and tell me what all this police activity is about.'

They rode the lift to the ward where Boris Stein had been placed and Jackson explained the reasons for the security.

'A dead cat?' Crawley said.

'Yes, sir. Poisoned by the same milk Mr Steen drank.'

'Stein. Is that official? Lab reports and so on?'

'No, sir. But it seemed to be a reasonable assumption. We didn't know that Mr Steen . . . Stein had . . . intelligence functions. Usually we've been informed.'

Crawley grinned and patted the young man's shoulder. 'Ted,' he said, 'some would deny that he has intelligence functions. He's a key-tapper, not a man of action like you and me.'

'Yes, sir.'

Boris was lying in a bed by a window. The afternoon light had an embalming effect—he looked small, shrunken, with his legs drawn up and his sparse hair flat on his skull. He was asleep, breathing regularly but lightly, and his features were arranged more peaceably than Crawley had ever seen them. The nervous, acne-scarred underslung jaw was at rest and the anxious, twitching eyebrows were still.

'Jesus,' Crawley said. 'He looks dead.'

Jackson shook his head. 'He's well out of danger.'

Crawley sighed. 'Wish I could say the same. You too, eh, Senior Constable? Gets pretty hot in Queanbeyan on a Saturday night?'

'Yes, sir. Sometimes, sir.'

Crawley backed out of the ward. 'Who else is in on this?'

'One of the Ds—Sergeant Clark, reporting to Inspector McNamara.'

'Okay. Now here's my contact number.' He clicked a ballpoint and scribbled on the back of one of Hector Bain's embossed professional cards. 'I want to hear about the analysis of the milk and the vomit and the shit. And in particular I want to know if the intention was to kill or disable. Got it?'

Jackson took the card. He had stopped sweating and had begun to warm to this solidly built aggressive individual who was obviously a professional, despite smelling slightly of alcohol and strongly of something else which Jackson couldn't place, although it was familiar.

'And if you or Detective Sergeant Clark run into any reporters,' Crawley said, 'print, radio, TV or whatever, what d'you say to them?'

'Nothing, sir.'

'Exactly,' Crawley said.

Ruth May's spirits fell after her confrontation with Dee, mainly because she was left in isolation for the next eight hours. She picked at the food, changed back into her tracksuit and even returned to sampling the *Reader's Digest*. She found the 'unforgettable characters' eminently forgettable and the 'humour in uniform' humourless. The lights went out early and she spent a long night in darkness, tossing and turning on the narrow hard bed. By first light she was desperate to urinate but her door-pounding produced no results. She squatted over the tray with its half-empty plate and bowl.

The morning dragged on slowly. She was frowsy and underslept, needed to clean her teeth and, despite the stink from the tray, she became hungry. She hammered on the door and got no result. *Great, Ruth*, she thought. *You've really taken the initiative*. The air-conditioner was turned off and the room grew first hot, then cold. By afternoon she became afraid that she had been left in the room to starve. She made a close examination of the sealed door and the barred window but found no possibility of breaking out. She lay on the bed, cried for a short time and fell into a restless sleep. She woke when the door opened. The older guard stood there, smoothing his silver hair.

'Miss May, my disappointment in you deepens. How can you allow yourself to get into such a state?'

'I'm being held here against my will. None of this is my choice. Why are you here moralising at me? Go away.'

'Interesting. You don't really mean that. You're desperate for human company . . .'

'You don't qualify.'

'And comforts. I imagine you're hungry and would like to clean up. I really don't want to make things harder for you than necessary.'

'Why don't you just kill me and be done with it?'

'Don't be stupid. Drop your bed linen on the tray. I'll take it away and then you can have a shower.'

Ruth's resistance crumbled. She stripped her bed and did as she was told. 'The other one said I could call him by an initial, Dee. What am I supposed to call you?'

'On the same principal, Tee, I suppose,' Gerard Thornton said. He took the tray and bed linen away and returned to escort Ruth to the bathroom. In the brief interval she took out the sheet of paper and tucked it inside the waistband of the tracksuit. The piece of crayon went into a pocket. She walked to the bathroom in a defeated shuffle with slumped shoulders, her head drooping.

'You'll feel better after a shower,' Thornton said. 'Take your time. Run a bath if you wish. There's plenty of hot water.'

As soon as the door was locked Ruth's shoulders straightened. She examined every item in the room for use as a weapon. Nothing. The shampoo was in a small, plastic bubble; the toothbrush was a tiny, disposable model that would break in a firm grip; all surfaces were smooth, nothing metallic or heavy was detachable. The window above the bath and shower was barred but open, nailed into place, a few centimetres open at the top to allow steam to escape. By standing on the rim of the bath Ruth was able to peer through the somewhat grimy window. The visibility was not good and the angle was difficult but it seemed to her that a brick wall ran along just below the window. It was built of different bricks from the courtyard wall—greyer, older.

Ruth climbed down, sat on the edge of the bath and removed the paper and crayon. She ran the hot water and hung the single towel over the keyhole. She wrote in bold capitals: HELP! I AM BEING HELD PRISONER IN THE HOUSE WITH THE WALLS. PLEASE ADVISE POLICE AT ONCE. MY LIFE IS IN DANGER. THIS IS NOT A JOKE. She signed in capitals 'RUTH MAY' and folded the paper as tight and small as she could get it. The hot water was mounting in the bath and steam was rising towards the window. She turned the tap off and climbed up again, balancing with difficulty on the slippery porcelain. She experimented several times before resting the folded paper on the top of the open window and flicking it out with her flexed fingers. It flew and dropped—outside the wall, she hoped.

She took off the tracksuit, ran some cold water and slipped into the bath. It was hot and soothing. She adjusted the two taps until the water flow was warm and washed her hair, then she ran more hot water and lay back in the full tub. *If I could wedge the door*, she thought, *I could stay here. There's water to drink and at least I can see out a little. I could wait until the police come.* She smiled at the thought. Tee would have the door off its hinges in no time. She watched her skin crinkle and thought about the younger guard. *Why isn't he around for me to work my feminine wiles on?* She climbed from the cooling water and towelled off. *Don't get into fantasy mode*, she thought. *It's a very long shot, but at least you've done something they don't know about.* She rubbed vigorously at her hair. It would be knotted and matted unless she could brush it. She didn't care. Maybe she'd ask for a razor on the next bathroom visit and shave her skull. Think how scary Robert de Niro looked in *Taxi Driver*. She found herself sitting on the edge of the bath, staring at the steamed-up mirror. *You're going nuts*, she thought. *Maybe this is what they want. Well, fuck them!*

Thornton's knock and voice were gentle. 'Are you decent, Miss May?'

Ruth almost giggled. She speculated briefly about her chances against Thornton in a physical encounter. He wasn't young and he had a limp. Perhaps she could catch him off balance. She remembered the man's imposing height and sinewy figure. She knew nothing about unarmed combat. Not a chance; and as for the feminine wiles . . . she looked at herself—pale, thin face, matted hair, shapeless tracksuit. Even Frank Hume wouldn't be interested. Forget it.

'Yes, you can open the door.'

She allowed Thornton to inspect the bathroom carefully, confiscate the towel and conduct her to the cell. He handed her a soft bristled brush and she sat on the hard chair and brushed her damp hair, left hand and right hand, until the strokes almost put her into a trance. Her arms ached and she felt very tired. She drank some water and wondered about the fate of her note. It was like putting a message in a bottle and tossing it into the sea. Worse. But such messages had been known to bring a response. She pulled the fresh sheets and blankets up and fell into a deep sleep.

~ 14 ~

'It's highly sensitive information,' Carol said.

Crawley clicked a ballpoint pen and scribbled a note on a pad. 'I'm a highly sensitive type of guy, Carol. Go ahead. Nice fast work, by the way.'

She had drawn the chair up close to Crawley's desk. The thin lips, still a little puffy, smiled. 'Thank you. I imagine there's more, but I thought you'd like to get something quickly . . .'

'Sure.' Crawley dropped the pen. 'Oh, did you get the fruit and stuff off to Queanbeyan hospital? For old Boris?'

'Oh, no, not yet. I'm sorry. I thought this had priority.'

'I want that done. And I'm expecting a message from the Queanbeyan police. Anything from them yet?'

Carol was thoroughly nonplussed. 'No, nothing at all. I don't think . . .'

Crawley watched her closely. She was agitated, but he judged it was his casual attitude to her researches, plus possibly a little post-coital confusion, that had thrown her. *She doesn't know how Boris was got out of the way.* He wondered how she would react to the fact of Boris's poisoning. 'It's okay,' he said. 'Might not be important at all. Right, what've you found out?'

Carol read from a printout. 'The three subjects—August Pope, Richard Beale and Beatrice Henderson—were members of an FSA unit long since disbanded.'

'Like the garbage collectors,' Crawley said.

'I beg your pardon?'

'Before your time. Go on.'

'It was variously named—the General Surveillance Unit, the Political Profiles Section, the Sample Survey and Analysis Desk. Its brief was to collect and analyse information on non-specific individuals and groups.'

'I'm not sure it's possible to have a non-specific individual,' Crawley said. 'But I get the idea. They spied on the citizens. Why not? It was all the rage back then.'

'The . . . GSU, shall we call it?'

'Let's not. Giving these things names tends to suggest they've got a right to exist. I remember hearing about that mob. It was done away with not long before I came in. They were the closest we got to an Un-Australian activities force.'

Carol was conscious that she was playing too passive a part. She glanced up sharply. 'I hadn't suspected you of being a bleeding heart liberal.'

'I'm not,' Crawley growled. 'There were some dopey people around then who could've made trouble, but by and large they were deluded and their own worst enemies. In most cases the best strategy would have been to give them return tickets to Moscow and Peking and a few free nights in the average Communist hotel. Instant cure.'

Carol retreated. 'I see. Well, Pope, Beale and Henderson worked together as a sub-unit, it seems. They dug up material of a highly sensitive nature.'

'You said that before.'

Carol flared. 'Am I boring you? I thought you wanted to hear about this.'

'I do. Sorry. Go on.'

She drew in a deep breath and rose from her chair. She approached Crawley, hooked a long thin arm around his neck and drew him into a kiss. Her tongue flickered into his mouth and her hand fell to his crotch. She bit his lower lip, drawing blood.

'Did that hurt?'

'Yes,' Crawley said.

'Good. I find all this exciting. Don't you?'

'All what? I've fucked smart, skinny women before.'

'I'm sure you have. I didn't mean just that. These people really dug about in the slime—adultery, divorces, adoptions, illegitimacies, incest. They got hold of medical information and were interested in religious affiliations and Masonic connections. I think they stumbled over some big, uncomfortable names.'

'Stumbled?'

Carol touched Crawley's bristly cheek and drew back into her chair. 'Wrong word, Raymond. They tunnelled in all directions. Must have had a lot of money to spend.'

'Nobody has ever called me Raymond.'

Carol tucked her blouse down into her skirt, achieving neatness and something more. 'It doesn't matter what I call you. What matters is these three people and Barry May.'

'And what was the association?'

'I don't know yet. I haven't got enough background knowledge to make proper assessments in some areas.'

'You're losing me, Carol. Background knowledge about what?'

'The FSA.'

'Assume the worst. Assume things are not what they seem. Assume deception and duplicity at the highest levels.'

'Are you serious?'

'Of course I'm serious. This is a secret organisation. Secret-keeping is addictive; once you start you can't stop. It's also destructive of loyalties and judgment. You'll see.'

Carol looked uncomfortable. She scanned another sheet. 'What you're saying has very serious implications in the light of this material. I'm only speculating, but . . .'

'Speculate,' Crawley said. 'Go on, speculate like mad. I want to hear it.'

'It's against all my training to do that. I'm an evaluator, a policy-maker.'

'Welcome to the reality of intelligence work, then,' Crawley said. 'It's mostly bullshit, fantasy and fiction, with just enough genuine nastiness buried in there somewhere to make it interesting. Think about Philby, what percentage of his life's activity had any real meaning?'

'I don't know much about him.'

'You should. In my book he was the most significant intelligence agent this century. Because of him, some people are dead and some are alive—but it was mostly just piss and wind. I'm sorry, I'm lecturing. Tell me what you think.'

'I think this kind of intelligence gathering went on later than people think. I don't believe that unit was disbanded when you say it was.'

'Interesting.'

'I'm sort of running with your ideas here, you understand?'

Crawley nodded, admiring the way she brought the proceedings back to focus on him. She was shrewd and combative, a dubious ally and a dangerous enemy. 'Push it a bit further. You're doing fine.'

'I suspect Barry May worked with these people and had access to the information they gathered. He may have sold it to . . . foreign intelligence services.'

Crawley smiled. 'Is that the worst idea you can think of? Come on, you're not trying. What if he blackmailed some of the people he had the dirt on—the Right Honourable what's his name, Lady whoever, Sir somebody something, Bishop this 'n that?'

Carol passed her pink tongue across her lips, which were dry and starting to crack. 'My god, is that possible?'

'Why not? Somebody snuffed him. Must be a reason. Your sort of speculation could be right or mine might be on the money. Who's still alive from the terrible trio?'

'Only Richard Beale. August Pope died in 1967 and Beatrice Henderson in 1971.'

'When everything was still running the way it had for twenty years. What've you got on Beale?'

'Nothing much. He's English.'

'That's one strike against him. You're not English, are you, Carol?'

'On my mother's side I am. My father's Greek.'

Crawley stared at her.

'Mainwaring's my married name. I'm divorced. Didn't you know that?'

Crawley shook his head. 'We're sort of reversed. My mother's Sicilian.'

'I know.'

Crawley cleared his throat. 'Back to Beale.'

'I ran into some kind of blocking code. I tried to get around it but I couldn't. I know he's still alive, but that's about all.'

'I told the archivist to clear all that shit out of the way. I thought we had an understanding on that.'

Carol drew a deep breath. This was the hard part.

'I don't know very much about that, but when I encountered this obstacle he was automatically alerted. I got a message.' She leaned forward and slid a sheet of paper across the desk towards Crawley.

'Advise the acting director and consult,' Crawley read. 'What the hell does that mean?'

'He wants you to communicate with his terminal as soon as I've given you all the data I have.'

Crawley grunted. 'It sounds obscene. Can you do that, please?'

She moved past him to the terminal, switched it on and began tapping the keys. Standing, slightly crouched, with her spine still straight, she looked like a perfectly poised golfer about to hit a copybook shot. She stood back from the screen to allow Crawley to see it. The message read: SUBJECT AREA HIGHEST RESTRICTION. SCHEDULING CONFERENCE MINISTER/BAIN/DACRE/RAMSAY/CRAWLEY 9.00 A.M. THURSDAY.

The semi-trailer had jackknifed at a bend on the highway a hundred kilometres north of Coota Coota. The load was highly toxic chemical solutions and one of the drums had ruptured. There was a danger of fire and explosion. This information was conveyed back, distorted and exaggerated, the length of the enormous traffic jam. Huck locked his van and tramped through the crush of protesting motorists, complaining children and worried environmentalists.

He stood a hundred metres from the crumpled, broken-backed wreckage and watched the undermanned police team as it struggled to keep people back. Three men sat under a tree with their heads on their knees. Huck used his bulk to hold back a man running forward with a video camera. A policeman nodded in appreciation.

'What's wrong with them?' Huck asked, pointing to the men under the tree.

'Exposed to fumes.'

'Where's the bloody ambulances?'

'Pushing through the traffic from both ends. They're in a bad way, those blokes.'

'I've got a four-wheel drive van with a bed in the back and I know the roads,' Huck said. 'With a bit of help from your lot I could get them to the base hospital pretty quick.'

The policeman shot Huck a look. 'You a cop?'

'I was. What d'you say?'

Another police car arrived and the man Huck had spoken to conferred quickly with his colleagues. The three stricken men were carried back to the van and two policemen cleared a path for Huck out of the congestion. He edged past other vehicles, knocked down scrub and drove on the wrong side of the road until he reached the first turn-off. Then he put his lights on high beam and picked up speed. Huck had explored the area in detail before deciding to settle on this part of the coast and the geography and road patterns were clear in his mind. The men lay in the back of the van, occasionally erupting into racking coughs, and Huck concentrated on whittling down the time and distance.

The police had radioed ahead from the crash site and he picked up an escort ten kilometres from Bateman's Bay. He drove up to the hospital with sirens wailing around him and blue lights blinking fore and aft. The hospital staff swiftly removed the men and Huck was given a cup of coffee. He was walking back to the van when one of the policemen from his escort stopped him. He held out his hand.

'You're a fucking good driver, mate. I'm Terry Cole.'

'Thanks, Sergeant,' Huck said. He shook Cole's hand but he was already planning an alternative route to Canberra.

'Sorry to do this, but they want you back at the crash. Seems more people have sniffed that fucking stuff and the ambulances can't cope. Will you be in it?'

Huck made three more trips to and from the site and was haggard with fatigue when he was finally discharged with thanks from Cole, who had been put in charge at the Bateman's Bay end. 'You've done a great job, mate. Could I have your name, please? I'd like to recommend you for . . .'

Huck's nerves were jagged from the prolonged, intensive concentration and associated caffeine overdose. He had to bite back a snappish response. 'Graeme Huck. But I'd be grateful if you didn't make any fuss, Sarge. I'm retired and I like a quiet life. Okay?'

'Whatever you say. Thanks again. They say that first batch you brought in are going to be all right. The quick delivery helped.'

Huck nodded and trudged towards his van, dusty and scratched, parked skew-whiff near the casualty entrance. He sat behind the wheel, smelling the sweat on himself and the odours left behind by his passengers. Several had vomited and at least one had urinated. 'Jesus, what a night.' He looked around and watched the last of the police cars pull away from the hospital. He took a half bottle of Johnnie Walker Red Label from the glove compartment, screwed off the top and took a swig. *This'll either knock me out or kick me on*, he thought. The whisky burned his throat. He found a Mars Bar in his jacket pocket and ate it quickly. He took another swig from the bottle. The glucose and alcohol kicked in and he felt a surge of energy. His vision was clear. He held out his hands, fingertips almost touching the windscreen. 'Rock steady,' he said. 'Canberra, here I come.'

He started the van and drove quietly through Bateman's Bay, monitoring his reactions, checking that he wasn't making the turns too wide or misjudging the distances. He was fine; he could probably take another slug somewhere around Braidwood without any risk. *Wouldn't do for the hero of the hour to be picked up DUI.* At the all-night petrol station he filled his tank, checked the oil and water and cleared the muck from the windscreen. He had a much-needed piss, washed his hands and face and felt fresh and alert. He bought another Mars Bar and chewed on it contentedly as he crossed the bridge and slowed to take the turn towards Canberra.

The traffic was light but there was a car ahead of Huck, not indicating a turn, and a truck behind him. A white car coming down the hill was stopped, waiting for the lead car to pass. Huck glanced indifferently at the car as it made the turn in front of him. The truck's headlights lit up the driver's face but Huck was a hundred metres around the turn and heading up the hill before the facts registered. *White car, lean, handsome face. Kiwi Draper!* He drove on, cursing, until he found a place to turn. His wheels spun in the gravel as he headed back down the hill, eyes straining ahead for a sight of the white car with the roof rack.

~ 15 ~

Ruth awoke, feverish. Her tracksuit and sheets were damp from sweat and there was an insistent ringing in her ears. She closed her eyes and fell back into a troubled drowse. Conflicting images danced and swung around in her brain—schoolteachers berated her (although this had never happened); a non-existent sister who looked suspiciously like photographs of her mother accused her of sexual activity with her father (another phantasm), and she struggled down a long corridor lined with bookshelves which shed their load in front of her as she moved.

Thornton hammered on the door. 'Miss May, Miss May! I have your breakfast.'

Ruth, jerked from a waking dream about the smell of chloroform filling her car as she drove, moaned and shouted. 'I'm sick. Go away. I don't want any bloody breakfast.'

The key turned in the lock and Thornton entered.

'Where's the breakfast?' Ruth said.

'On a tray outside the door. You don't think I'd be silly enough to walk in here with a tray in my hands, do you?'

Ruth lay back on her pillow and wiped sweat from her face with the edge of the sheet. 'I don't give a fuck what you do. You've probably poisoned me.'

'Don't be ridiculous.'

'Why not? This whole thing is ridiculous. I'm nobody. I don't know anything, except far too bloody much about Rory Michael Broderick.'

'Who?'

Ruth laughed until she felt her strength give out.

She shut her eyes. A cold shiver ran through her overheated body. 'Go away. Let me die.'

'You're being melodramatic.'

Ruth didn't answer. She was slipping back into the warm, irresponsible world of dreams. Crawley, dark and sceptical, wearing incongruous grey kid gloves, floated somewhere between Thornton and the door. He bent over her bed and touched her face but the hand was hard and rough like a chunk of bark. Then she felt suddenly cool. The bedclothes seemed to dry underneath her and she was grateful for the change. The ringing stopped and she felt soothed as if a major problem had been satisfactorily solved. She fell into a deep, untroubled sleep.

Thornton was standing by her bed when she woke up. If she had dreamed she had forgotten the content, but she still felt rested and secure. For an instant the feeling shaped her consciousness and she thought she might be somewhere else, out of the tiny, oppressive room. But the illusion quickly vanished.

'You again,' she said.

'I'm afraid so. I trust you're feeling better?'

'I am. What did you do?'

Thornton shrugged. 'Nothing much. A sponge bath and some injected medication. The textbook says you will experience thirst.'

Ruth was aware of a throat-seizing dryness. 'Yes,' she croaked.

Thornton produced a glass of water and held it for her to drink. The liquid was cool and delicious. She relaxed back on the dry pillow, aware that she was naked. He must have stripped off the sodden tracksuit. She didn't care. *He wouldn't nurse me if he was going to kill me*, she thought. She looked up and smiled. 'Thank you.'

Thornton's expression was amused. He took a sheet of paper from his shirt pocket and unfolded it. 'I thought you might like to have this back. It's yours, I believe. I found it just outside the wall when I did my routine inspection.'

Ruth looked at the paper, read 'HELP! I AM BEING HELD PRISONER . . .' and turned her face into the pillow.

Derek Ramsay and Rupert Dacre walked by the lake. A three-man BNA field team kept watch at a discreet but effective distance. The sky was overcast with a threat of rain. Ramsay carried a furled umbrella, which he held by the ferrule while he swished at leaves with the crooked handle.

'Satisfied?' Dacre asked.

'Mm. I'd like to know what Crawley's thinking.'

'Mrs Mainwaring doesn't seem to be in too much doubt about that.'

'Women have been known to overestimate their influence with Crawley—his wife, for instance. But that's by the by. I think things are moving ahead acceptably, yes.'

Dacre glanced nervously back at the man walking twenty paces behind him. 'Is this really necessary? This spymaster stuff?'

Ramsay smiled. 'Probably not, but these people have to be employed somehow. I must say it amuses me. You'll have to get used to it, Rupert, if you're going to mount the ladder.'

Dacre nodded and looked out over the choppy grey water. He was recalling Carol's animated verbal report—the life in her dark eyes, the movements of her slender body. Disturbing images but intriguing ones.

The woman clearly found power an aphrodisiac and that offered interesting possibilities.

'Rupert?'

'I'm sorry,' Dacre said. 'Did you say something? I was . . .'

'Not wool-gathering, I trust. The next step is going to require a performance from you. You realise that?'

'Indeed. And just how much do we tell Hector?'

It was Ramsay's turn to be distracted. He flicked at a skipping leaf and demolished a small anthill with nervous swings of the umbrella. He had had a report on the indisposition of Ruth May, competently handled by Thornton, but nothing as yet from Draper. He had no intention of telling Dacre of these developments, but they were on his mind—potential dangers, potential opportunities. He pulled himself back to the here and now. 'As little as possible. I've had some news from London. Hector's contributions have been unimpressive to say the least. His star is on the wane, Rupert.'

Dacre's imagination filled with visions of the advantages to be gained from heading up a government security agency and a private company. It had the smell of the future about it, obviously, and he could see his own career as the stuff of textbooks. Such prizes, however, were for the taking, not the accepting. 'What about Crawley?' he said. 'Wouldn't he be a strong candidate? Especially if there's a change of minister? I hear Mortlake's favoured if there's a reshuffle and that he and Crawley once played on the same football team.'

Ramsay laughed, genuinely amused. 'Really, Rupert. You're carrying information-gathering too far. If Mortlake and Crawley played on the same team it's

123

likely Crawley flattened him at some time or other. Besides, Mortlake won't get it. Our man is safe in the saddle. Trust me.'

'His seat's a bit marginal, but at least the election's a long way off.'

'I have to get back,' Ramsay said. 'There's a lot to do. I take it your preparations are well advanced— documents, videos and such?'

'Yes. I suppose Crawley will show up?'

Ramsay took a savage swing with the umbrella, which flew from his hand and described a perfect arc. He caught the handle and gave a grunt of satisfaction. The old rumour about Crawley, Huck and the late Toby Campion flitted through his mind. Directors of the FSA had come and gone and Crawley was still menacingly in place. But surely past his best these days. Screwing Carol Mainwaring, installing the May woman in the Lake Royal. Absurd mistakes. Recollection of the smooth, assured, economical moves of Gerard Thornton comforted him. 'I feel confident that Ray Crawley's star is on the wane, too,' he said.

'Inspector McNamara on the line, sir,' Carol Mainwaring said.

'Switch him through,' Crawley said. 'Any word on Hector?'

'Due in tonight.'

'Dr Dacre's on the ball. Carol, straight after you put the inspector on would you please go and get me some aspirin? I've got a hell of a headache.'

'Hello, Mr Crawley is it? Kevin McNamara, Queanbeyan CID here.'

'Would you hold on for a second, Inspector? Thanks.'

Crawley put the phone down and moved quickly from his desk to the door. He opened it quietly and saw Carol Mainwaring still sitting in her swivel chair. From the inclination of her head he guessed she was listening to the conversation with the broadcast volume turned severely down. 'Carol, I really need the aspirin. D'you mind?'

'Of course not.' She flicked a switch and got up, grabbing her purse from the desk.

Crawley watched her pass into the outer office before going back to his desk. 'Sorry, Inspector. You're calling about my bloke in the hospital?'

'That's right. You want the lab report?'

'If it's in English.'

The policeman chuckled. 'I'll translate it for you. Mr Stein was poisoned. A puncture was found in a milk carton. Someone injected his lite white with something pretty nasty. Killed the cat outright.'

'This is important, Inspector. Does the report indicate whether the dose was intended to kill a human or just make him sick?'

'Hang on, I'll try to make sense of all this scientific mumbo-jumbo. Blah, blah, here we go . . . "Mr Stein's weight is estimated at only fifty-two kilos, which accounts for the severity of his response." Response, shit, what a word. "An average adult Australian male can be expected to weigh seventy kilos. At such a weight the dose intensity is suggestive of an intent to cause serious gastric disturbance rather than death." Not much comfort to Mr Stein.'

'But useful. Thanks, Inspector. I'd be grateful if you could keep all this under wraps.'

'I understand. A prosecution is unlikely, I take it?'

'Very.'

'Mr Stein's residence wasn't on our register. I'm not saying it would have made any difference, but . . .'

'Mr Stein's away with the fairies most of the time. Could you keep an eye on his place while he's in hospital?'

'For sure.'

'Thanks for your help, Kevin. And your blokes Jackson and . . .' Crawley reached into his memory, 'Cloke, Clark . . . have done a good job on this. I'd like to buy you a drink some time. We're in your debt.'

'I hear you, Mr Crawley. Good day to you.'

Crawley hung up and leaned back in his chair. The headache was genuine. He had spent the night in a hotel room with Carol Mainwaring, drinking more than was good for him. He had told himself he was working, probing at one of the layers of deception that made up what he was thinking of as the Barry and Ruth May matter. He knew this was only partly true. The hormonal rage he had experienced the first time with Carol Mainwaring wasn't something he could ignore. Like most men of his age, Crawley was aware of the waning of his sexual interest and powers.

But the pale, narrow, whippy body that had excited him so much the first time had failed to stir him again, and he had used alcohol, partly to stimulate his desire and partly to explain and excuse his decreased ardour. He sat behind his desk with his head throbbing and his mind in turmoil. The complicity of Carol Mainwaring was the only handle he had on the broader aspects of the problem, but it was an emotional and professional minefield. His thoughts drifted away to consideration of Huck's investigations and the involvement of Kiwi Draper. No result so far from the search for the New Zealander. An image of Ruth May came into his mind, followed by one of Mandy.

He was groaning and holding his head when Carol Mainwaring came into the office. She placed a glass of water and three aspirin tablets on the desk. 'Here you are. Is there anything else I can do?'

He shook his head. Carol Mainwaring went back to her desk and rewound the tape she had made of Crawley's conversation with the Queanbeyan policeman.

~ 16 ~

Huck picked up the white car, which he identified as a Honda Accord, several kilometres past Bateman's Bay. The Honda was moving fast, staying just inside the speed limit, and Huck had trouble keeping it in sight. His van, although well maintained, lacked speed. *Kiwi always was a hoon*, Huck thought as he wound the van up for an attack on a long hill. A siren wailed behind him and he stayed left to allow the police car to pass. As he topped the hill he saw the Honda take a bend, not as far ahead as he would have expected. The highway patrol car had evidently reined Draper in a bit.

Huck took another swig from the Johnnie Walker bottle and concentrated on holding a steady enough speed to keep him in touch with the Honda. The driving was easy, compared with his dashes to the hospital, and he relaxed, allowing cars to pass him and provide cover as he headed south. He worried about not being able to alert Crawley to the involvement of Gerard Thornton but he judged it to be more important to track Draper. He was sifting through impressions and speculations as he drove. One was uppermost: *What was the reason for Kiwi coming down here again*? To search Barry's house? Unlikely. Coming back to the scene of a kill was a risk a hitman rarely took. Huck had to conclude that Draper's most likely target was himself.

A few kilometres north of Narooma fatigue hit Huck like a mailed fist. The reflectors along the edge of the road seemed to blink at him. He realised that his eyes were closing and he was missing every second one. He struggled to stay awake but the winking reflectors and the broken line on the road were like a countdown to sleep. He slowed, thinking that to break the rhythm of steady driving might help. It did, but only for a short time. At the slower speed his head grew heavier as the tyre and engine noise lulled him. Cursing, Huck turned on the radio and stabbed the buttons, searching for music. He got a flickering signal from an ABC relay station—a Pacific Islands news broadcast. Huck acknowledged defeat. He pulled off the road at the first opportunity, set his watch alarm and crawled into the back of the van to sleep.

Dawn woke him before the alarm. The cold light flooded into the van as the sun rose quickly out of the sea. Huck yawned and almost gagged when the smell of sweat and vomit reached him. He scrambled out with his stomach heaving. In the open air he felt immediately better. A fine, clear day was building. He ran his hands through the grass and wiped the dew over his face. Grunting, he performed a few slow callisthenics. The breeze was fresh and his skin tingled. He climbed back into the van, packed and lit his pipe, and drove on.

Huck knew from his long experience of hunts, chases and stakeouts that he had lost a significant advantage by being forced to take a break. Following an alert and trained person was much harder than it appeared, but it was still preferable to searching for him. Still, if Draper was headed for Coota Coota and Huck was his target, the odds swung in Huck's favour. He'd be on his home ground with Toby as a formidable ally. Against that were the constraints of the law, which Draper did not have to consider, and another big plus for the Enzedder—his youth.

The sun was well up when Huck reached the outskirts of the township. He calculated that Draper had about two hours' start—not long to scout around a very out-of-the-way house and approach it with extreme caution, which was certainly what he'd do. Huck drove through the back lanes and parked behind the pharmacy. A short whistle brought Toby bounding from the yard behind the shop. The big dog allowed Huck to pat him before he sniffed cautiously around the van. He stood with his tail thumping the driver's door while Huck thanked the pharmacist, who confided that he wanted a pup from a litter sired by Toby.

'I'll arrange it,' Huck said.

He let Toby into the front passenger seat and drove off. The dog's nose twitched at the smell coming from the back of the van. Huck stopped behind the general store and walked through a vacant block to the street. He looked carefully around, checking the wharf, the petrol station, the parking spaces near the pub and post office—no sign of the Honda. In the store he bought a carton of milk and two corned beef sandwiches. Toby growled as he watched his master eat and drink. Usually the dog would get a crust or two at the least, but Huck gave him nothing. He wanted Toby hungry.

Huck's route to his house was circuitous and painstaking. First, he eliminated certain old roads and tracks that Draper, if poorly instructed, might have stumbled down by accident. That done, he was left with the obvious approaches—by land or by water from either the north or the south. Nothing he knew suggested that Draper was a boatman and, in the off-season, there were no boats readily for hire. Huck crossed the water approach off his list. He could have enquired in the township about strangers asking for his whereabouts but he was unwilling to take that step. If he found Draper he might have to kill him and it would be better that no one made any definite connections between them.

Huck left the van concealed in thick scrub a kilometre from his house. He put two spare magazines for the MP40, a pair of binoculars, the whisky, a hunting knife and five metres of light cord into a canvas backpack which he shrugged on. The gun he slung over his left shoulder so that it sat above his right hip, ready for quick use. He was wearing blue jeans, old R.M. Williams boots, a grey flannel shirt and a zippered nylon jacket. He rubbed dirt onto his bristled, sweaty face and adjusted the sit of his olive green baseball cap. 'Okay, Toby, old son,' he said. 'Let's go hunting.'

Huck found the Honda in the scrub. It was well concealed if you happened to be doing your looking at ground level. But Huck had surveyed the ground from a high bluff, using the glasses, making careful sweeps. He worked his way down to the scrub patch and admired Draper's handiwork—tyre marks brushed out, no signs of cut branches in the immediate vicinity, natural-looking leaf scatter. More importantly, he concluded from the smell and heat retention of the car that it had been hidden not long before. A few hours at the most.

The Honda wasn't locked—no need to lock something that wasn't there—and the keys were in the ignition. Huck checked the car carefully for a booby trap before removing the distributor cap and putting it in his bag. He moved cautiously down the track with Toby at his heels. The dog sensed the need for quiet and confined itself to buried growls. Two hundred metres from the house Huck left the track and scouted in wide arcs to right and left, using the cover—scrub, outcrops of rock and overgrown rubbish middens—that he knew so well. He lifted the binoculars from time to time, adjusting the focus, probing dark recesses, but saw nothing. His hand skipped nervously to the MP40 to feel the comforting, oiled solidity of the chunky magazine and the folded stock.

Closer to the house, Toby began to growl insistently. He scratched at the dirt and lifted his head to make muted bays of protest. Huck's large hand closed around the dog's muzzle. 'What is it, boy? What the hell's the matter?'

Toby stopped growling and moved ahead with his legs bent, his nose closer to the ground, hackles rising. They were less than a hundred metres from the house now with only a thin cover of gnarled and stunted banksias between them and the back door. Huck sat down behind one of the bushes after sweeping aside its dropped cones. Toby hunkered down with him. *I don't like this*, Huck thought. *He's down there, in the house or nearby. But there's something wrong.*

Crawley's attempts to telephone Huck had failed. He had heard nothing from Mandy in Melbourne. The only news of any kind he had had was bad: the Queanbeyan hospital had reported that Boris Stein's condition had worsened suddenly, that he was fighting a severe infection and had been placed on the critical list. Crawley found himself in the kind of position he hated—supposedly at the centre of things, but totally inactive.

Carol Mainwaring brought him a steady stream of negative information: Dr Dacre and Derek Ramsay were unavailable. Crawley phoned Lyle Davis, a former journalist, now a political staffer in the attorney general's office, with whom he'd had secretive dealings in the past, but Davis knew nothing about the meeting with the heads of the intelligence services.

'Are you trying to tell me something, Creepy?' Davis asked.

'No, for Christ's sake. I'm trying to find something out.'

'You sound rattled. I thought you were the great Pooh-bah over there for a while.'

'Great bullshit shoveller. So you've seen or heard nothing about intelligence matters in the last day or so?'

'Just the usual. Mostly this flak about the fifty-year rule. Your man's pushing that *real* hard. Harder than any of the others.'

'My man? Who would that be?'

'Dacre, the archivist. Hey, I did hear a whisper about him, now I come to think of it. I didn't pay much attention at the time. An archivist, after all. It sounded silly. What's it worth?'

'What d'you want?'

'I'll tell you when I want it.'

Crawley considered. Writing Lyle Davis a blank cheque was inviting trouble but he was desperate for something to grapple with. 'Okay, Lyle.'

'I heard that this Dacre character is after Hector Bain's job.'

Crawley hung up and switched on his computer. His self-proclaimed computer illiteracy was partly a pose, partly a ploy. He disliked using the things and much preferred for others to use them for him, but he had mastered certain basic skills. He tapped in the code to protect his enquiry being accessed by another terminal and ran the program that would give him 'ground level' access to the personnel files of members of the intelligence services. Accessing the so-called 'basement files' would involve more complex procedures, which would have tested Crawley's patience. He hoped to find what he needed on the ground floor. He did; the search revealed that Rupert Dacre and Derek Ramsay were both members of the Yarralumla Bridge and Social Club.

Crawley grinned. 'A crime in itself,' he said. He consulted the telephone directory and dialled the number listed for the club.

'Bridge club.'

'This is Derek Ramsay.' Crawley did his best to imitate the BNA man's fruity tones. 'Would Dr Dacre happen to be there, by any chance?' It caused him almost physical pain to pronounce the last word with a long 'a' but he did it.

'Just a minute, sir. I'll see.'

Crawley whistled tunelessly through his teeth as he waited.

'No, sir. Dr Dacre isn't in the club.'

'Not in our usual spot?'

'No, sir. Shall I say you called if he comes in?'

'Not necessary. Thank you so much.'

The Tiberius of the telephone, Crawley thought sourly as he hung up. He paced around the office pondering the information: *Dacre, Ramsay, Hector, the minister, maybe—all after something. What? And in some way connected with the death of Barry May. How?* No answers came.

He was still pacing when Carol Mainwaring came into the office. She had put on and buttoned the tight, checked jacket that matched her straight skirt, and was carrying her handbag. She advanced warily towards Crawley, who leaned back against his desk.

'I want you at that meeting tomorrow,' he said.

'Certainly. I wondered if you had any plans for tonight.'

'Why change a good plan?'

Colour mounted in her pale face. She came closer and he could smell her peculiar fragrances—the almost astringent skin lotion and something softer in her perfume. It occurred to him that he had never had an affair so dominated by smells. He reached for her and kissed her hard. She responded fiercely, dropping her bag, throwing herself into the embrace like a snake striking.

'Good,' she said as she broke away. 'I've got something to do later in the night though.'

They went in separate cars to the same motel. In the tavern next door they had two drinks and steak sandwiches. Carol Mainwaring scarcely touched the food. They went to the room and stripped the bed and each other in swift, excited movements. Two strong gins had an alarming effect on the metabolism of the forty-five-kilogram woman. She shook with passion as Crawley entered her and orgasmed violently almost at once. Crawley, his response muted by the alcohol and the condom, ploughed on until he realised that Carol Mainwaring was asleep and in danger of being crushed by his insistent weight. He withdrew, rolled off and lay on the bed thinking of Mandy. *She's screwing someone in Melbourne for sure. Who? What does it matter?*

Crawley pulled a sheet over Carol Mainwaring and himself and tucked a pillow under her head. She was breathing regularly, dropping occasionally into a light snore. He drowsed. A beeping noise woke him. She was climbing out of bed, looking at her watch, glancing at him. Crawley watched her through lowered eyelids. She found her underwear and slipped into it. Crawley, detumescent but unsatisfied, felt a throb of desire as she zipped up her skirt and slipped into her shoes. She bent over the bed and kissed him on the cheek.

'You were great,' she said. 'See you at the meeting tomorrow.'

Crawley grunted and rolled over. He was up from the bed and pulling on his clothes as soon as the door closed behind her. He heard her car start and was out, unlocking the BMW and firing up the motor while her rear lights were still showing in the street. She was driving a fairly new Nissan Pulsar and driving it well, Crawley noted. He followed at a distance, slipping easily into the light stream of traffic. Very quickly it became clear that she was headed for the airport. Crawley relaxed and tooled along comfortably in a clutch of cars behind her. He allowed several other vehicles to precede him into the carpark and stopped seventy-five metres away from the Pulsar. A light, misty rain was falling. Carol Mainwaring locked her car, tucked her keys into her bag and tapped along quickly on her high heels towards the terminal doors.

Feeling frowsy, with his digestion misbehaving, Crawley slouched into the terminal at the other end and worked his way back. It was after nine p.m., with very few flights due in and out. Still, there were enough passengers, airport staff and expectant wives, husbands and lovers to provide cover. Crawley lurked behind a bookstand and watched Carol Mainwaring, alert as a worm-seeking bird, glance around the arrivals lounge. A tall, distinguished-looking type with smooth grey hair and a florid complexion joined her. Crawley recognised Derek Ramsay. He moved along to a position behind a display of ACT tourist brochures so as to get a better look out on the glistening tarmac.

He let out a small snort as he saw Hector Bain, briefcase in hand, poplin raincoat over his shoulders, stride into the terminal to be greeted by Ramsay and Carol Mainwaring.

~ 17 ~

Ruth May had ignored the cut on her leg. Now she became aware that the Elastoplast had lifted and that the wound was itching. Her fingers strayed to it. A thick scab had formed. Her mind a despairing blank, she plucked at the scab with the long nail of her index finger. It was dark outside with rain pelting at the window. *Another day gone. How many more could she stand before she . . . did what? There was nothing to do.*

The corner of the scab lifted and blood oozed out, quite a lot of blood. She was sitting on the bed wearing the top of the tracksuit. Her legs were bare. She formed a mental picture of herself as she plucked idly at the scab—thin and pale, half naked, wild-haired, like a crazy woman from a Victorian novel. The idea came to her in a sudden rush. She peeled off the tracksuit top and examined the metal zipper. Then she tore the scab from the scratch. Blood welled out. She dabbed her fingers in it and smeared it across her face. When the blood stopped flowing she gouged at the wound with the catch of the zipper until she got a fresh supply. She dug deeper, ignoring the pain, and the blood flowed strongly. She streaked it across her shoulders and breasts. Pulled the lips of the scratch apart, got more blood, and repeated the process until she was daubed reddish-brown from forehead to navel.

She hammered on the door.

'Yes?' Thornton's voice was cool, untroubled.

'I have to shit,' Ruth said. 'Let me out or I'll do it here and wipe it on the wall. Do you know that Chuck Berry song. Tee?' She sang loudly and off-key:

We did it in the kitchen
We did it in the hall
I got some on my finger
So I wiped it on the wall
'You are disgusting, and you sound hysterical.'
'So would you be if your fucking bowels felt like mine. But yours froze shut years ago, didn't they?'
'Stand back!'

Ruth took a deep breath. The door opened and she allowed Thornton to get one look at her war-painted face and body before she charged, arms raised, fingers extended, screaming. She aimed her rush at Thornton's limping left side and caught him precisely with her full weight. She slammed him at hip height and he lost balance, spun away, hit the wall. Ruth went past him with a whoop and dashed into the corridor, which had several passages leading from it. She had no idea of the best direction to take and she cursed herself for not thinking about this beforehand. She kept moving, avoiding the one direction she knew—towards the toilet and courtyard.

She burst through a door into a sitting room, ran through that and found herself in a large, flagstoned kitchen. She could hear movement behind her. She snatched up a carving knife and clawed at the heavy bolt on the door. Thornton lunged at her and she slashed at him with the long-bladed knife. Backhand and forehand, instinctively doing the right thing, instead of stabbing, which Thornton might easily have turned aside. He was surprised at the ferocity and accuracy of her slashes. One caught him high on the arm, slicing through his shirt and drawing blood. He sagged and another swipe bit into his shoulder.

The bolt slid open and Ruth was out in the cold

air. It was very dark and raining but she ran headlong into the blackness over gravel, grass and hard ground. She bumped into trees and fought through bushes, tripped and fell, pulled herself up and ran on until her wind gave out and she lay gasping and shivering on the cold wet earth.

Huck was puzzled. Draper must have discovered by now that the house was empty. What was keeping him there? True, there were things of interest in the place— some expensive bugging equipment and fishing gear, a few weapons, a substantial collection of pornographic comics and videos. It seemed unlikely that Draper was sitting down to read *Rape Planet* or watch *Cuntrabandits* or *Poking Fun*. Huck scouted three sides of the house, keeping at an even distance of about sixty metres—the effective range of the MP40. He retreated further away into the dunes to get a look at the sand- and salt-blasted front porch, door and windows, but the result was the same—no movement.

Setting a booby trap seemed to be the only explanation, but would Draper seriously think Huck would fall for that? Briefly Huck considered the possibility that Draper had seen him at the crossroad out of Bateman's Bay, was aware that Huck had followed him back and was now lying in wait inside the house. He dismissed it. The Honda driver had been looking the other way and the cab of Huck's van could not have been illuminated.

Huck returned to the best cover, the banksias at the back of the house. 'Come out, you bugger,' he whispered.

Toby, hunkered down beside him, growled.

Huck watched the back door open, as if in answer

to his demand. Draper, wearing a dark tracksuit, gym boots and a knitted wool cap, came and stood in the shadow cast by the overhanging roof. A neat, compact figure, he looked carefully around, seeming almost to be tasting and sniffing the air. Huck put his hand on Toby's head, keeping them both very low, quiet and still. Through the leaves and the high grass he saw Draper nod as if satisfied, go back into the house and re-emerge dragging a large plastic bag with his right hand and carrying a shovel in his left. He propped the shovel against the door jamb, looked around again and, reflexively, touched his left armpit.

Gun under there, Huck thought. *Bloody hard to get at with a garbag and a shovel to carry.*

Draper bent and lifted the bag easily onto his shoulder. He picked up the shovel and began to walk up the track. Twenty-five metres short of the spot where Huck and Toby were hiding the track branched to left and right. Draper took the right fork, heading up towards a scruffy patch of ti-tree, she-oak and black boy struggling to survive on the edge of the dunes a half kilometre from the house.

Huck waited until Draper, moving easily despite the obvious weight of his burden, was fifty metres ahead before rising slowly from his hiding place. Scrub and pampas grass grew high along the track and cover was not a problem. Nevertheless Huck hung back. He might never get a better chance to surprise Draper while keeping all the odds on his side, but curiosity to know what the New Zealander was about made him decide to wait.

Caution was the order of the day. Huck kept Draper in sight and advanced on the left flank, observing the old military rule that right-handers, alert for enemies, look first and hardest to the right and left-handers to the left. Draper stopped several times and looked back. Huck and Toby froze. The dog appeared to be enjoying the stalking game, but Huck knew its patience would eventually run out and it would dart at a bird breaking cover or snuffle after a running lizard. He moved more quickly, gaining ground on Draper, who was struggling a little as the track grew rougher and the incline more steep.

Eventually Draper reached the spot he had selected. The area was a last patch of vegetation, gaining moisture from the lie of the land and the protection of a bluff, before the dune grass took over.

Had a good look round before he went to the house, Huck thought as he took up a position behind a thin-trunked casuarina. He had expected nothing less of a professional. Draper had dumped the plastic bag unceremoniously in front of him, stepped to one side and peeled off his tracksuit top. He wore a singlet and a quick release pistol-harness. He dropped his right gym boot firmly onto the shoulder of the shovel, digging it into the sandy soil.

Huck moved up quickly to the left, circled behind Draper. He waited until the spade was deep in the ground again before approaching with the machine pistol cocked and levelled. 'Stay exactly where you are, Kiwi. Foot on the spade, that's right. I've got a gun here that'll cut you in half if you move your hands.'

Draper relaxed, holding the handle of the spade. He eased up a little but kept his foot in place, balancing easily. 'Huck?'

'Right, you careless prick. Toby, go!'

The dog jumped forward and crouched, snarling with his teeth centimetres from Draper's crotch.

Draper jerked the spade towards the dog and his hand flew towards the holstered pistol. But Huck was prepared for the move; he kicked Draper at the base of the spine. The heavy, reinforced toe of the boot connected with a solid thud and the New Zealander collapsed as the shock wave ran through him. Huck used his knife to cut away the shoulder harness. He picked it up, noted that the gun was a serviceable 9mm automatic and shoved it into his bag. Draper moaned and rolled over. Toby had dropped into a quiet, watchful stance.

'You'll be all right, son,' Huck said. 'Better a kick up the bum than Toby biting your balls off.'

'Fuck you.'

'Waste of breath, Kiwi. When you feel a bit better I'll get you to open the bag.'

'Open it yourself.'

Very deliberately Huck put his right heel on Draper's outstretched left hand. He let his weight come down until two fingers broke with sharp cracks. Draper screamed and Toby barked sharply. 'Open the bag.'

'I can't move.'

'Toby!'

'Okay, okay.' Draper crawled towards the bag, using his right hand to grip the grass and dirt and dragging his twitching legs. Suddenly he rolled, turned and threw a handful of dirt up at Huck. But Huck had seen Draper's fingers close around the dirt and had moved quickly to the right. The dirt sprayed harmlessly.

'You're game,' Huck said. 'I'll give you that. I'd bust your other hand but I've got work for you to do, I suspect. Open the fucking bag, Kiwi, and stop pissing around.'

Draper reached out and scrabbled at the knot that held the bag closed. He got it undone and let the bag gape open.

'Pull it down a bit, slowly.'

Draper pulled and a man's head and shoulders came into view—thin shoulders, beanstalk neck topped with scruffy, carroty hair.

'Put your face in the dirt,' Huck said. 'Toby, watch!'

Huck kept the MP40 trained on Draper's inert form while he put his boot under one shoulder and turned the body over. The head flopped loosely. The mild, guileless eyes of Reggie Carmichael stared up at him. The mouth was slack, with just the suggestion of a foolish smile.

'Jesus,' Huck said. 'Why?'

'You ought to thank me. I found him at your place. He was going to rip everything off.'

'Bullshit. Reggie wouldn't know how. Didn't you realise he was the local halfwit?'

Draper shrugged and rolled over. He winced as his broken fingers took some pressure.

'You tried to get him to tell you where I was,' Huck said. 'And the poor bastard didn't know because I was careful not to let him see me leave.'

'What does it matter? A fucking defective. One less in the world for the all-there people to support. Right?'

'You're still trying, aren't you, Kiwi? Still hoping I'll get careless and make a wrong move. Forget it. Your number's up. You might just like to know that it was this bloke who put me onto you and Gerard Thornton.'

'Bullshit.'

'Thanks. Thornton it is.'

'I didn't say a thing.'

144

'You didn't have to. Reggie here saw the two of you talking to Barry May. Told me all about it.'

'What are you going to do, Huck? I could've done you before at May's house, remember?'

'And you would have if you'd been told to. Me, I'm not going to do anything. But you're going to bury my mate here.'

'I can't dig with this hand.'

'Yes, you can. The ground's soft. And dig it pretty big, Kiwi. I'm keeping my options open.'

Huck squatted while Draper worked. The New Zealander was strong and fit and he dug efficiently, despite the damage to his hand. Huck examined the Smith & Wesson model 39. A heavy gun, which only an expert could use well. He trained it on Draper's perspiring back. The New Zealander appeared to sense something. He stopped digging and turned.

'Huck . . .'

'Finish the hole.'

A proper send-off with flowers and a bullshit speech by some minister who didn't know him wouldn't mean anything to Reggie, Huck thought. *Better to do it like this with Toby and me here. And it's not a bad spot either.* Besides, he didn't have time for the police and all the formalities, and he couldn't just leave Reggie here for the bandicoots and dog packs.

Draper slowed and wrung his hand.

'That's enough,' Huck said. 'Tie him up and put him in.'

With difficulty, Draper did it.

'Fill it in.'

'I need a drink. I'm fucking dry.'

Huck took the whisky from his bag and allowed Draper to take a long swig. He kept the machine pistol centimetres from his temple. Draper shovelled the earth back into the hole and stood. 'Fair enough?'

'Stones,' Huck said. 'Big ones. From the beach.'

'Have a heart.'

Huck lifted the muzzle of the pistol. 'He's buried because he was a harmless, decent bloke, not a piece of shit like you.'

Draper worked for half an hour carrying stones from the beach and laying them over the freshly dug earth. It was a poor, untidy job and he collapsed before it was properly finished.

'Huck,' Draper gasped. 'I've got something to trade with.'

'Thought you might, Kiwi,' Huck said.

~ 18 ~

Perversely, Crawley wore a suit to the meeting. He had shampooed his hair and tamed it, shaved closely and found a recently dry-cleaned shirt in a drawer. His silk tie was dark blue, bought in Saks on Fifth Avenue, New York City, a gift from his daughter, Vanessa. He had drawn the line at the matching pocket handkerchief. He went patiently through the security procedures before being escorted to the conference room. Carol Mainwaring, in dark suit and severe blouse, looked shocked when she saw him.

Crawley grinned. 'We look like the Bobsey twins.'

'They're in there,' she hissed.

'Cheer up, love. They're only men with dandruff, tinea and bad breath, just like everyone else.'

'You're cheerful this morning.'

'I slept well.'

It wasn't true. He had gone back to the motel after following Carol to the airport, unwilling to endure the loneliness of his house. His sleep had been restless and he'd got up early, driven home and gone about his elaborate toilet and dressing partly to put domestic thoughts out of his mind.

'Do you have . . . instructions?' Carol Mainwaring said.

Crawley shook his head. 'No. I take it Hector's back?'

'Yes. I saw him just now. I came back out to wait for you.'

'Cat's back, end of mouseplay. Let's go in.' Crawley ignored the look she shot him and held the door open for her.

The room was the one Dacre and Ramsay had met in some days before. Both were there now, Dacre sitting primly at the table, Ramsay sprawled languidly in a half-turned chair. Hector Bain, looking pale after his spell in London, rose to his feet. Dacre and Ramsay acknowledged the woman's presence with small shiftings and head-bobbing.

'Ray,' Bain said, advancing with his hand outstretched. 'I hear you've done a marvellous job. I must say you look the part.'

Crawley merely smiled and shook Bain's hand, noting the trademark impeccable tailoring and accessories. Bain's outfit made his own not inexpensive suit look like something off the peg. He watched the director usher Carol Mainwaring to her chair and nodded at Ramsay and Dacre. 'Derek, Rupert. Good morning.'

'I think you should take the chair, Derek,' Bain said smoothly. 'All agreed?'

Nods from Crawley and Dacre. Ramsay swung around and shifted the chair so that he was looking directly across at Crawley. Bain and Carol Mainwaring sat to Crawley's right; Dacre was on the other side of the table one chair away from Ramsay. A considerable number of papers was spread out in front of him, making the gap look neither subservient nor impolite.

Ramsay cleared his throat and fingered the notepad in front of him. 'Apologies from the minister. Cabinet crisis or some such nonsense. At the outset I should say that Mrs Mainwaring's security clearance has been upgraded to enable her to be present at these proceedings. She has worked closely with Dr Dacre and Mr Crawley on this matter and . . .'

'And with myself,' Hector Bain interjected. As a

matter of policy he was unwilling to allow himself to be excluded in a preamble.

'Quite. Moving on . . .'

'Just what is this matter? Just what are these proceedings?' Crawley said.

Ramsay frowned. 'Really, Crawley, I think we must prefigure . . .'

Crawley took off his jacket, undid his top shirt button and slipped down the knot of his tie. 'Bullshit, Derek. Don't waste your breath. We've got two dead, a missing woman, a colleague in hospital close to death and a bloody New Zealand hit man going round taking pot shots at a former member of the FSA. That's all the prefiguring we need.'

'I imagine it's a little more complicated than that, Ray,' Bain said.

Crawley leaned back in his chair and put his hands on the table. Carol Mainwaring stared at the hands. They were large, thick-fingered, rough, but she remembered the gentleness they were capable of. She glanced at their owner, unable to conceal the admiration she felt at the way he had so far dominated the meeting. Rupert Dacre observed her reaction and covered his distress by consulting a sheet of paper. Crawley pretended indifference, but missed none of the by-play. He eased his wedding ring back. 'Tell me,' he said.

Ramsay exchanged a quick uneasy look with Hector Bain before speaking. 'It appears,' he said, 'that Hopkins and May had gained access to some . . . sensitive files and were blackmailing certain people. We have independent corroboration of this.'

'In the form of?' Crawley said.

Dacre passed a sheet of paper to Ramsay. 'The

journalist, Kelvin Mahony, is apparently on the scent of something. He . . .'

'He's a stooge,' Crawley said. 'He's anybody's.'

'He's an author,' Dacre protested. 'An investigative journalist with an international reputation.'

Crawley snorted. 'You haven't been in this business long enough to judge, doctor. Reputations can be bought and sold, manufactured, manipulated. I've got a reputation as a ruthless operative. It's based on half a dozen incidents in a twenty-year career. Mostly, I've just sat on my arse, like you.'

'Ray,' Bain snapped, 'being offensive won't help. Clearly, when we're aware of the dimensions of the problem . . .'

Crawley grunted. 'I'm glad something's clear to you.'

'Clearly,' Derek Ramsay waved expansively, 'there is, out there, a malevolent force bent on eliminating certain threats to its well-being.'

Crawley rolled up his sleeves. 'I can't believe I'm hearing this. Okay, okay. I don't buy it. Nothing I've ever heard about Barry May fits this picture. But, let's say that's true. Who gives a bugger? Blackmailers are filthy little worms, right? The fewer the better. Somebody did everybody a good turn.'

Dacre passed another sheet to Ramsay. 'I'm afraid you're missing the point, Crawley. Our analysis of the data suggests that there may be more such blackmailers. Indeed . . . I hesitate to use the word on account of its sensationalist connotations, but . . . an organisation.'

'This analysis is news to me,' Crawley said. 'I hope you've been kept abreast of it, Hector?'

Bain did not respond.

'Go on, Derek,' Crawley said. 'You're in the chair, after all.'

Ramsay slammed his hands on the table. 'I've had about enough of you, Crawley. There is nothing, so far as I am aware, on the record from you about a poisoned colleague or a hit man. I suggest you're dramatising, perhaps manoeuvring to stay in Hector's chair a little longer.'

Crawley fixed his gaze on Dacre. The archivist blinked, glanced at Carol Mainwaring and looked down at his papers. Crawley lifted his hands from the table and spread his arms. With his wide reach he seemed to encompass Carol Mainwaring and Hector Bain like a victorious football coach embracing try-scorers and goal-kickers. 'Go ahead, Derek,' he said. 'Give us what you undoubtedly will call your scenario.'

Nothing had gone according to plan for Derek Ramsay, Rupert Dacre or Carol Mainwaring apart from Hector Bain's obvious bewilderment. Sensing the lack of support, Ramsay was forced to plough ahead with his script. He said: 'As you are all aware, there was a time when organs like the FSA and the BNA collected data on private as well as what we might call public citizens. Not to be indelicate, some of that data is marital, medical and psychological and has the power to inflict great harm on individuals, families and organisations today.'

'Absolutely,' Dacre said.

'The deaths of Hopkins and May and the investigations of Mr Mahony indicate the potency of that information. Our first priority is to reduce that potency. In this area Dr Dacre is the expert.'

Hector Bain's immaculate appearance masked a bad case of jet lag compounded by total confusion. He had

151

been led to expect a routine meeting—a handing-over of the reins by Crawley, perhaps with some resistance. Also a report from the archivist, plus a little polite liasing with the BNA. Now, he appeared to be in the middle of a deep policy and practice discussion on matters about which he was almost wholly ignorant. Why hadn't Carol briefed him properly? And when did Rupert Dacre start holding hands with Derek Ramsay? Even more disturbing was something he sensed about Carol Mainwaring. Sitting beside him, she seemed almost to be generating heat. Last night at the airport he had been shocked at the change in her appearance. The ice woman had melted. Now she was dissolving. *Crawley*, Bain thought. *The bitch is fucking Ray Crawley. She's changed sides and the two of them are after my job.*

'First principle,' Dacre said, 'information which cannot be published or broadcast is immediately devalued.'

'What does that mean?' Crawley said.

'It means that if the data in our files is protected by a two-generation rule then its usefulness to a blackmailer is enormously reduced.'

'*Sixty* years?' Carol Mainwaring's plucked eyebrows shot up towards her strained hairline.

Dacre smiled. 'Exactly. Given the circumstances, the legislation can be framed so as to make the publication of protected material a criminal act. I was hoping to be able to advise the minister this morning . . . Well, no matter. There's plenty of support for the two-generation proposal.'

'Has a nice historical ring to it,' Crawley said.

Dacre nodded. 'Absolutely. Furthermore, experience in the States has shown that freedom of information legislation is the thin end of the wedge into secret intelligence.'

'I quite agree,' said Bain, struggling. 'But we've got that already.'

'The legislation to introduce the two-generation rule can also contain provisions excluding the information so protected from all FOI requests, thus providing an extra level of security.'

'You know what they'll say if you get behind this, Hector?'

Bain was distracted, watching Carol Mainwaring watching Crawley. 'No, what?'

'They'll say you were protecting your dad. Wasn't he involved in some big FSA fuck-ups back in the fifties?'

'You're being ridiculous,' Bain said.

'You mean you're in favour of this *sixty*-year bullshit? And getting exemption from FOI? The journos'll tear you apart.'

Bain was flummoxed. 'There is that aspect to consider.'

'Bet your arse there is,' Crawley said. 'Is this the best you can do, Derek? Put a padlock on the stable door after the horses've reached the hills? C'mon, Rupert. What about all that computer power? Every man, woman and dog that's ever worked for the FSA and the BNA must be on file. You should be able to spot these dastardly blackmailers. Especially with Kelvin Mahony on the team. Spot 'em and clobber 'em. What d'you say?'

Dacre looked helplessly at Ramsay, who had never before lost control of a meeting so badly. Hector Bain was a born waverer, but he knew when to jump. 'I agree,' he said crisply. 'Long-term proposals are all very well but the situation seems to call for action. Rupert, I suggest you get to work as Crawley suggests. Try to devise a profile of the . . . mis-users and get a match-up with the personnel files. If you have any trouble get back to me. I met a terribly clever chap in London who knows all about this sort of thing. I could get him out on a consultancy if need be.'

Rupert Dacre bowed his head and collected his papers. Carol Mainwaring looked at Ramsay, giving him his chance.

Ramsay pushed back his chair. 'What Crawley proposes is simplistic. I think this thing will prove to have roots and tentacles. I'll be in touch, Hector.' He closed his virgin notepad, pocketed his pen and walked from the room.

'So,' Hector Bain said. 'A pretty little mess I've flown back to. Carol, I think you could've briefed me.'

'Carol's been busy,' Crawley said. 'Was there something else, doctor?'

Dacre shook his head. He put his papers in a tooled leather briefcase and followed Ramsay.

When the door had closed behind the archivist Bain turned to Crawley. 'What the hell was that all about?'

Crawley stood and slung his jacket over his shoulder. 'What did Carol and Derek tell you at the airport last night?'

Carol Mainwaring stiffened. 'You followed me. You got up out of bed and followed me.'

'They told me you were thinking about trying to take my job,' Bain said.

'I hope you didn't believe them, Hector. I'd rather spend the rest of my life at a Khamal concert than take your job.'

'I see.'

'There's a lot going on you don't know about. Somebody poisoned Boris Stein and took a few shots at Huck.'

'Oh, Jesus, no,' Bain said. 'Don't tell me Huck's involved.'

''Fraid so, Hector. We'd better go somewhere and have a long talk.'

Carol Mainwaring rose from her chair. 'Mr Bain, I should . . .'

'Sorry, love,' Crawley said. 'Too late to change sides now.'

~ 19 ~

Huck marched Draper back to the house, gave him some aspirin and handcuffed him to the massive combustion stove which sat, unused since Huck's occupation, in the corner of the kitchen.

He sat at the table, poured himself a whisky and packed his pipe. He had Draper's Smith & Wesson in front of him and the distributor cap from the Honda. He held up the cap. 'Just in case you think you've got the strength to lug the stove up the track.'

Draper sneered and ran the handcuff along the rail of the stove until he could sit comfortably, with his fists on his knees. 'Very funny. What about a drink and a smoke?'

Huck puffed the pipe. 'Very bad for a man in your profession. Slow you down.' He examined the automatic. 'Good gun. This the one you used on Charles Rawlins? I heard that kill was credited to you.'

'Are we going to talk shop or really get down to it?'

'I'm not sure. Barry May was my friend, you see. Best friend I had around here.'

Draper shrugged. 'Everybody's somebody's friend. It was just a job.'

'Like the one in Tasmania?'

'I'm not saying another fucking word until we talk about a deal.'

'You talk.'

Draper stared at the rough board floor, then let his eyes drift up over the walls to the ceiling. 'This place bugged?'

'That's the least of your worries.'

'Who said I'm worried?'

'Listen, Kiwi, I can take you out there in a boat and drop you over with a hundredweight of metal around your neck. Or I can do you here and now and feed you to Toby a piece at a time. Who'd know or care?'

'And you'd still be in the dark and in the shit.'

Almost casually, Huck lifted the automatic and fired. The report seemed to rock the house and the bullet missed Draper's head by centimetres. It ricocheted off the stove and exited through the wooden ceiling.

Draper sneered again. 'So you can shoot straight. Big deal. Means nothing.'

'Tell me about Ruth May,' Huck said quietly. 'Barry's daughter. I know you snatched her.'

That was reaching, but Huck was interested in Draper's reaction and he got what he was hoping for. The New Zealander's defiant stare dimmed fractionally and a look of uncertainty flitted across his regular features.

Got you, Huck thought. *That's your ace in the hole.*

'I don't know anything about her.'

Huck got up and strolled around the kitchen. He could see signs of intrusion—jars and packets out of place. Reggie Carmichael had probably come in to nick some food or grog, nothing more. Suddenly he felt his temper rise as the adrenalin he'd been running on for hours cut out. He walked to the stove and planted a hard kick in Draper's ribs. Draper's breath rushed from his body and he sagged back against the cold cast iron. Huck put the muzzle of the pistol against his temple. 'Tell me where she is, Kiwi. Tell me everything about it. Or I swear I'll be rowing you out to sea in ten minutes from now.'

Draper struggled to draw in a tortured breath. He looked up at Huck. 'I didn't kill your mate. Thornton did. Take it easy with that thing. It's old and unreliable.'

'So am I.'

'As for the defecto, I didn't mean to kill him. I only gave him a tap. He must've had a weak neck, crook vertebrae or something.'

'You're not telling me anything I want to hear.'

'Listen, Huck. You're right. I know where the girl is. Thornton's got her. But you won't get near the place without me and I want some guarantees.'

Huck backed off to the dresser, found a plastic cup and splashed some whisky into it. He handed it to Draper who juggled it in his free hand. 'Thanks. I knew you'd see sense.'

'All you've got so far's a few fingers of scotch. Don't make a big production of it.'

'Look, I don't know what all this is about. Haven't a clue. But Thornton does. He reports in, not me. He knows who's calling the shots.'

'That's very thin. You must know something more than that.'

Draper gulped some whisky. 'It's coming out of Canberra. That's all I know.'

'The girl's being held in Canberra?'

'In the bush, not far away. That's all I'm saying. Shoot me if you want. Unless I get a deal I'm dead anyway.'

'What kind of a deal are we talking about?'

'What d'you reckon? Immunity. A ticket out. What else?'

Huck said nothing. He opened a can of dog food and went out to feed Toby. The dog was gambolling in the backyard, gripping a length of rope in its jaws and swinging it around and bucking like a rodeo horse. It gave the rope a last flick and trotted over to where Huck was scraping the food into a bowl. He patted the dog and made a routine inspection for ticks as it ate. He filled the water bowl and shook out the blanket on which Toby slept under the house. It was almost dark and Huck was tired and hungry. He didn't fancy a night of Draper's company but he knew he wasn't up to driving to Canberra without some solid sleep. He went back inside to find the New Zealander working at the padlock with a nail he'd pulled out of the floor.

Huck took the nail away. 'Only works in the movies,' he said. 'Did you see *The Silence of the Lambs*?'

Draper shook his head.

'Don't sulk, Kiwi. Things are going your way.'

'What d'you mean? My fucking hand hurts.'

'I'll put a splint on it in a minute. I mean I'll talk to someone in Canberra about your proposition.'

'Who?'

Huck crossed to the phone. 'Ray Crawley.'

Draper frowned. 'Crawley. That bastard! I thought he'd retired, like you.'

'I can't even imagine it,' Huck said. He dialled Crawley's number and listened to the ring for a full minute.

'Out on the piss,' Draper said.

'Shut up.' Huck pressed the re-dial button and got the same result.

'So what now?'

'I'm going to make some food and have a sleep. Get an early start.'

'What about me? You're not going to leave me here all night?'

Huck located some surgical tape and snapped some straight sticks from the kindling he kept near the open fire in the living room. He had Draper lie on his face, handcuffed his wrists behind his back and applied a rough splint to the broken fingers. Draper swore several times during the operation but did not resist, for which Huck was grateful. He was deeply tired and might have had difficulty subduing Draper if he had found a surge of strength. He restored the New Zealander to his previous position, gave him some more whisky and set about heating cans of soup and toasting bread. They ate in silence. Huck tried Crawley's number again without success. He looked at his watch. 'Anything more to say?'

'Not a word.'

'Wouldn't Thornton be expecting some kind of a report? Like on how you blew my brains out? Or were you thinking about a house fire?'

'No comment.'

Huck yawned. 'Okay. Time for bed.'

Draper was sitting on the floor with his back to the stove. 'I can't sleep here.'

'Why not?'

'It's too fucking cold for one thing.'

'Tell you what. I'll give you a choice. Would you rather I sling you a blanket or light the oven?'

Ruth May was not a countrywoman. She disliked the bush and had been relieved when her father had decided to settle on the coast rather than inland. Beaches and coastal scrub she could cope with, mountains and forest depressed and alarmed her. When she awoke after escaping from the house and losing consciousness she was at first so terrified by the dark and the thick press of vegetation that she did not feel the cold. Then she shivered and she began to shudder. The rain had stopped and there was no wind but the air seemed to be like an icy bath. She was still clutching the carving knife and she experienced one second's satisfaction at the memory of cutting her guard, making him bleed, stopping him. Then the shuddering became uncontrollable. If she lay here she would die.

She stood and stumbled forward, crashed into a thick bush and fell on soft, wet grass. She used the knife to hack branches from the bush until she had enough to cover her. She lay down and pulled the thick, leafy branches over her. She curled up, seeking warmth by clutching herself into a ball. *People survive like this in the snow*, she thought. Unbidden, one of Rory Michael Broderick's alleged exploits came to her—the occasion when he had hidden from Mongolian bandits in a snow mound and emerged none the worse for wear. She laughed and felt herself on the brink of hysteria. Would Tee come looking for her? Miserable as her situation was, she was determined that he wouldn't find her. She clamped her chattering teeth shut and thought about warmth—log fires, doonas, thick socks, hot coffee. After a time, she felt herself growing hot. Then she drifted into a feverish sleep.

'Dacre's after your job, Hector,' Crawley said.

'That's absurd. He's an archivist, for God's sake. He hasn't had the experience.'

'You haven't exactly been a hotshot field man yourself. Make no mistake, these technocrats are trying to take over. But this isn't just about jobs.'

'What then?'

Crawley looked across at Carol Mainwaring. They

were in Hector Bain's office and it was a measure of the seriousness of the occasion that Bain had taken no note of the disturbances to the decor Crawley had initiated. He sat behind his desk looking undernourished and worried. Crawley was standing by the window. 'I wonder if Mrs Mainwaring can help us?'

'Carol?' Bain said. 'I thought you were loyal to the FSA, if not to me personally. What are you doing . . . conspiring with Derek Ramsay?'

Carol's brain was humming. Everything had gone wrong. Crawley had steam-rollered them all. She'd underestimated him badly, but surely she could salvage something out of this? It shook her that he'd been able to follow her to the airport when she'd thought she'd left him in a sexual stupor. The incongruous thought struck her that there was a calculating, using capacity in Crawley that she associated with the feminine psyche. Strange, to be beaten by the feminine side to a man like Crawley. It shook her confidence, but she decided that there was nothing to gain by retreating.

'I have been . . . romantically involved with Mr Crawley. I admit it. I also believe that he was angling to secure permanent appointment to the directorship. I was alerted to this by Mr Ramsay. I'm afraid that's all I have to say.'

Hector Bain spread his hands on the desk and examined his manicure. 'And what about Dr Dacre? What was the expression? You were working in close conjunction with him?'

'Dr Dacre is a senior officer of the FSA. I did what he instructed me to do.'

Bain raised an eyebrow. 'Which was?'

'Convey archival information to Mr Crawley.'

Crawley pushed off from the window and flopped into a chair. 'This is going in circles. They got Boris out of the way so she could feed me this stuff about blackmail. My guess is that it's all bullshit.'

Carol Mainwaring stiffened. 'I don't know anything about what happened to Mr Stein.'

'I hope not, for your sake,' Crawley said. 'Derek Ramsay's the man, Hector. He's been having little meetings with Dacre at some club they belong to.'

Bain looked distraught. 'I can't mount any kind of attack on Derek. He's head of the BNA.'

Crawley grinned. 'Which branch of the service has the most clout? Wouldn't you like to find out?'

Bain groaned. 'God, no.'

'I would,' Crawley said.

Bain's phone buzzed. He flipped a switch and said, 'No calls.'

The phone was on broadcast. 'This is for Mr Crawley. It sounds extremely urgent.'

Derek Ramsay's knuckles whitened as he gripped the phone. 'What do you mean, she's gone?'

'Just that. She got away last night.'

'And you wait until now to inform me.'

'I've spent the whole bloody night looking for her. She wounded me with a knife.'

'How did she get a knife? Don't answer, I don't want to know. How well equipped was she?'

Thornton's voice was faint on the scrambled line. 'She was naked and ill. There's a good chance she's dead under a tree somewhere.'

'Naked. You weren't . . .'

'No. Nothing like that. She's a clever woman with

163

a sense of the dramatic. I was careless, I admit it. The point is . . .'

'To find her,' Ramsay said, 'and bury her. Do you understand me?'

'Of course.'

'What have you heard from Draper?'

'Nothing, but I haven't exactly been standing by the phone.'

'Get busy,' Ramsay said. 'I don't suppose I have to tell you, Gerard, that this isn't going at all well.'

~ 20 ~

Huck slept late. Toby was patient but eventually barked to be fed. Huck, in pyjamas and with his feet shoved into laceless sandshoes, shuffled out to the kitchen to find Draper, blanket-wrapped, sitting with his back to the stove staring out the window.

'I'm dying for a piss,' Draper said.

Huck kicked a plastic bucket across the floor. He disliked speaking or being spoken to before he had had several cups of strong tea. He took a bag of dry food from a shelf and went out to feed the dog. The morning was bright and crisp but the heavy dew was already beginning to lift. Huck swore when he realised how late it was. He quickly filled the bowl and gave Toby a pat. 'Lucky you didn't get a rabbit,' he growled, 'or I'd still be asleep.'

Inside he plugged in the electric jug, shovelled tea into a pot and filled the four-slice toaster.

'Early start, eh?' Draper jeered.

'Shut up. Push the bucket across slowly. Any bullshit and I'll make you drink it.'

Draper moved the bucket. Huck filled the teapot and slapped butter and plum jam on the toast. He poured a cup, added milk and drank it scalding hot in a couple of gulps.

'Mine's white with two.'

Huck poured tea into a plastic mug and put it, along with two slices of toast, within Draper's reach. Then he poured more tea for himself and picked up the phone.

'I don't care who he's with or what he's doing,' Huck barked. 'Tell him it's Huck and it's fucking important.'

Draper watched as Huck packed his pipe and lit it, puffing out clouds of smoke.

'How can you do that first thing in the morning?'

Huck swallowed tea and puffed while he waited impatiently. He pointed the wet stem of the pipe at the New Zealander. 'Save your breath. Pretty soon you're going to have to do some real talking.'

Hector Bain winced as Huck's voice filled the room. Crawley elbowed him aside and positioned himself behind the desk. 'Creepy? Huck. Listen, I've got Draper. He's confirmed he was in on the kills. Claims not to know what it's all about.'

'Who does?' Crawley snapped.

'According to Kiwi here, Gerard Thornton knows. Remember him? BNA bloke? Retired.'

'I know him. What else does Kiwi say?'

'He knows where the May woman is and he wants a deal.'

'What kind of deal?'

'The usual—immunity and a ticket to Bali. He says she's being held in the bush somewhere near Canberra. That's all he'll say.'

'Have you tried persuasion?'

'He's got a couple of broken fingers, bent ribs and a sore backside. Plus he's spent the night on the kitchen floor. He's said all he's going to say for the time being.'

'Tell him if the May woman survives I'll personally put him on a plane to Auckland. If she doesn't I'll bury him in the Brindabellas.'

Carol Mainwaring's narrow, slanted eyes opened wide as Crawley spoke. She was pale and her bottom lip trembled. She trapped it between her teeth and looked at Hector Bain.

'Really, Crawley,' Bain said. 'You simply haven't the authority to . . .'

'Shut up, Hector, and start getting a team together. Four, I'd say, and none of your civil liberties types. Hucky, we need the name of the place.'

Huck communicated the substance of Crawley's message to Draper, then used a match to pick his teeth. 'The name of the place where you've got Ruth May. Just the name.'

'Not much of a deal.'

'It's give and take.'

'Thistle Creek,' Draper said. 'Near there.'

Hector Bain nodded. 'I know it. A friend of mine has a property out there.'

Crawley scowled. 'How nice. Where is it?'

'South, towards Cooma. Somewhat off the beaten track, though.'

'One-horse town, big place, what?'

'Spread out, I'd say.'

'Great. Okay, Hucky. How soon can you get there?'

'Here to there,' Huck said. 'How long?'

'Depends on the driver and the vehicle.'

'Don't piss me around. And give us a meeting point.'

'Two hours, give or take thirty minutes. There's a bridge over the fucking creek.'

Huck looked through the open door to the next room, squinting to see the time on the VCR clock. 'Be there by 1 p.m., Creepy. At the bridge.'

'Bring Toby,' Crawley said, 'and bring every bloody gun you've got. I remember Thornton better now. Very big on ordnance, as I recall. Great work, Hucky. See you soon.'

Hector Bain was talking urgently on another line when Crawley hung up.

'What about me?' Carol Mainwaring said. 'I don't understand anything about this.'

Crawley was shrugging on his jacket. 'I believe you, Carol. What was it for you? A job jump?'

She nodded. 'I was promised a job at . . .'

'I don't want to know. Tell you what, if Boris Stein pulls through I'll see you right. How about that?'

'Oh, my god.'

'Why don't you go out to see him. Why don't you nurse him back to health. Know what I mean?'

'You're disgusting.'

'Aren't I? Hector, how's it looking?'

'I've got Peter Hallows and two others.'

'That'll do. Pete'll love this.'

'I hope you know what you're doing, Crawley.'

'So do I. We've got a minute. Wasn't Gerard Thornton in line for Derek Ramsay's job?'

'I believe he was, yes.'

'Interesting. They seem to be getting along now.'

'What do you mean?'

'Come on, Hector. This is all some kind of inter-agency bullshit. There's someone or something to protect.'

'I haven't the faintest idea . . .'

Crawley took off his tie and put it in his jacket pocket. He bent, opened the bottom drawer in the big desk and took out a .38 Ruger automatic. 'Carol?' he said. 'Any ideas?'

Carol Mainwaring sprang from her chair and ran from the room. Crawley released the spring holding the pistol's magazine. The slim metal box jumped into his hand. 'I'd put someone on her tail if I was you, Hector. Queensland to a banana, she's headed for Derek Ramsay or Rupert Dacre.'

Bain picked up the telephone and spoke urgently into it. When he hung up he turned back to Crawley, who was looking out over the lake again. 'What are you really hoping to achieve? If it's an internal matter . . .'

'External people are dead and in danger,' Crawley said. 'I happen to think that's wrong.'

Ramsay watched with distaste as Carol Mainwaring lit a cigarette. He smoked an occasional cigar himself but disliked seeing women smoke.

'I'm sorry,' she said. 'But I need it.'

Ramsay nodded. He touched a button under his desk, turning on an extractor fan. The woman was fighting to gain control of herself in a way that Ramsay admired. Perhaps she would prove to have more gumption than Rupert Dacre, who had been uncontactable since the disastrous meeting ended. 'You said it was urgent.'

After two long drags, Carol Mainwaring butted the cigarette. 'It is, I'm sure, although I don't know what it means . . .'

'Perhaps if I knew what it was?'

'Who is Ruth May?'

'That does not concern you.'

'It concerns Crawley and that dreadful creature Huck. They know where she is.'

'What?'

She told Ramsay everything she had learned in Bain's office. Ramsay listened in silence. When she had finished he picked up the telephone and stabbed the buttons angrily. He got no answer and slammed the receiver down. 'Fuck it!'

'Would you please tell me what's going on?'

Ramsay smiled. 'You want to know what move to make next, do you?'

'Yes, of course.'

'Of course. Did Crawley have any suggestion?'

She shook her head. 'Just something . . . awful.'

Ramsay stood. 'I advise you to adopt it. I'm afraid I have to leave now.'

'You can't just walk away. I haven't got anything out of this. I've probably lost my job. Oh, god . . .'

'You are a slut, Mainwaring, nothing more. You make a slut's choices and you must expect a slut's reward. But there is one service you could perform.'

'Why should I do anything more for you?'

'Oh, not for me alone, for yourself. Locate Rupert Dacre and tell him to keep his nerve, that is if he has any nerve to keep. Also to shut his mouth. Do you understand?'

'No, but what does that matter? How can it help me?'

'Dacre, now—you might try switching your affections to him.'

Carol Mainwaring straightened her skirt as she stood up. Some hair had escaped from her tight arrangement and was straggling over her face. She felt untidy and dirty. 'You're as bad as Crawley.'

Ramsay nodded. 'I'm afraid you've fallen in with a very bad lot. Now, if you'll excuse me, I have things to attend to.'

Ramsay watched her walk from the room, then he lifted his briefcase from the floor, extracted some papers and spread them across the desk. He glanced out the window and took a belted raincoat and an umbrella from a stand. He called for his car to be brought to the front of the building. His secretary looked at him inquiringly as he passed her desk. *Don't tell me that Mainwaring bitch has got her claws into old Derek*, she thought.

'You can reach me in the car,' Ramsay said. 'For anything very urgent.'

The secretary nodded. *Doesn't mean a thing. His car's big enough to do it in.*

Huck gave the back of the van a quick clean and put Draper inside, passing the handcuff chain behind a bolt that held the spare wheel in place.

'Toby, in, boy!'

The dog jumped up into the van and lay within easy snapping distance of Draper's ankles.

'Wouldn't move around too much if I was you, Kiwi. Toby's not a real good traveller.'

'This van fucking stinks. What've you had in here, Huck? Dead fish?'

'Sick men. You'll survive, but the smell won't improve Toby's temper. Just shut up and get ready to tell Crawley everything he wants to know.'

Huck moved the armoury from the back of the van to a place under the front passenger seat and put an unfolded map of the Cooma district on top of the seat. He had a thermos of whisky-laced coffee, two fully packed pipes and matches within easy reach. It worried him slightly that he couldn't see Draper but he felt confident of the handcuffs and Toby. He started the van and drove up the track away from his house, away from the hidden Honda, away from poor Reggie's grave. It felt good to be going on a field operation with Crawley again. But he knew from experience that that good feeling mightn't last.

~ 21 ~

Carol Mainwaring was told that the chief FSA archivist had gone 'to look at pictures'. She found Dacre in the restaurant attached to the National Gallery. He had an untouched rice salad in front of him and was two-thirds through a bottle of red wine. She sat down opposite him and poured some wine into a water glass.

'Mrs Mainwaring, hello.'

Dacre's thin hair clung limply to his skull and his face was pale and drawn. Carol Mainwaring realised how much she despised men in general—Dacre, Ramsay, Bain. All promoted above their capacities and performing on a par with their abilities. She drank some wine. 'What are you doing here, Dr Dacre?'

'Rupert. Odd name isn't it, Rupert? I was named after Prince Rupert, nephew of Charles I. Lost several battles in the English Civil War. Fitting, wouldn't you say? My dad was a history nut, you see.'

'Rupert, then. Derek Ramsay . . .'

Dacre lifted his glass. 'Don't mention that man to me. Got me into this awful mess. I see that now. Entrap . . . entrapment. Probably same thing happened to Prince Rupert, poor bastard.'

Carol decided to take another tack. 'I wish I knew what this was all about. I thought it had to do with jobs, you know—promotions, for you and for me.'

'No, no. Not really. Only partly. You don't want to know what it's really about. Far too silly.'

'Silly? You say silly? People have been killed and kidnapped, and you use the word silly?'

Dacre's eyes focused intently. 'What are you talking

about? Dead? Kidnapped? I haven't the least idea of what you mean.'

'I believe you,' Carol said soothingly. 'But that just goes to show how much we've been used. Several people have been murdered and a woman is being held prisoner somewhere. Oh, yes, Crawley's friend Huck has a prisoner as well. Crawley proposed torturing him to get information.'

'My god!'

'And Boris Stein has been poisoned. What are you doing?'

Dacre was struggling to his feet. 'I have to get away. Out of the country. This is dreadful.'

Carol Mainwaring reached across the table and pulled Dacre back down into his seat. He was drunk and off balance but her strength surprised him. 'Listen,' she hissed. 'All I have to do is get to a computer and I can block your passport and your credit cards. I can alert Interpol.'

Dacre was pale and sobering fast. 'Why on earth would you do that?'

'Because I don't want to be left holding the baby. Now tell me what it's all about. Quickly!'

Dacre told her, giggling at one point and waving his hands about. Carol listened impassively. She had not imagined that her estimation of men could sink lower but she found it happening. She drank some wine but Dacre was in full flight and ignored his glass. When he fell into self-justification Carol told him she'd heard enough.

'What are you going to do?'

'I don't know.'

'You won't do what you threatened?'

'I can't see how it would benefit me.'

'God, you're hard.'

'Go away and let me think. Everybody seems to have an escape route or a deal worked out except me.'

~ 22 ~

Ruth May heard Tee moving through the bush. His limp made it difficult for him to move quietly. She lay still and listened, praying that she was completely covered. The noises, leaves being disturbed, branches being pushed aside and broken were alarmingly loud, dangerously close. For an instant she was afraid that he was going to step on her. She held her breath. Then the sounds were past her and moving away. She had no idea of the time, having fallen in and out of feverish dozes through the night. She hadn't had the energy or will to move when it got light. She was grateful for that non-disturbance of her cover now. In one lucid moment she had panicked at the thought of being lost in the bush. That danger was past and she knew what to do. She rose slowly from the grass, let the branches and leaves fall away and, still clutching the knife, she followed Tee. She did not know how far she had run when she escaped from the house. Surely not far, but in what direction? Sooner or later Tee would have to go back there, and that was where she would find food and have a chance of getting help, somehow.

She was cold, wet, scratched and bruised and her muscles were stiff, but she ignored the discomfort and moved on, keeping Tee in sight, catching glimpses of him through the scrub. His noise would drown hers. He did not seem to be looking around, which puzzled her until she realised that he must be on his way back after a fruitless search. Good. She wondered how badly she had wounded him with the knife and drew closer to get a better look at him. He appeared to be wearing a sling to support one arm. That was good, too. The sun was climbing in a pale sky. It was intensely cold but she was still feverish and the concentration on keeping the man in sight and not making excessive noise helped her to ignore it. She envied him his leather jacket, though.

Suddenly her prison was in sight. The house appeared to rise straight up out of the bush, the high wall notwithstanding. It was a stucco building, constructed on different levels on a sloping site. For some reason the word 'villa' came into her mind although it was hardly appropriate to the setting. The outer wall enclosed a couple of hectares of bushy garden and the main gates were standing open. By sheer luck she must have run through the gates instead of into the wall. The bastard was overconfident, she thought, to leave the gates open. She hid behind a tree and watched the man trudge through the gates and up a path towards the house. He looked tired and defeated and she remembered that he wasn't young. He also had a limp and was wounded. Her spirits rose until a violent shuddering overcame her. She slowly collapsed, drawing her knees up and resting her face on her crossed arms. She was freezing cold and sick. The odds weren't good.

There was only a rough dirt track leading from the house. God knows how far away a main road was. She was sure she'd never make it naked and on foot. The house was her only hope. She forced herself to stand up and withdraw into the scrub. She circled wide towards one long side wall and approached it cautiously. The wall seemed to grow higher as she got closer. It was smooth and topped with barbed wire. She'd never get over it. She felt despair overwhelm her and slid down, shivering and close to hysteria. Then she heard an engine start, rev up and idle. She could see clouds of smoke rising from behind the wall. She crept through the high grass towards the gate and saw a Mercedes back out onto the road. Tee wrestled clumsily with the steering wheel, made the turn and drove away. Ruth dashed through the gates towards the house.

She went through the front door and the enveloping warmth almost made her dizzy. She forced herself to think. She needed clothes and a telephone. Kidnappers had to have a telephone. But the house was so big. Clothes first. She didn't want Tee to know she'd been back so she couldn't recover her tracksuit. She ran upstairs to a mezzanine that had several rooms off it. In a closet she found an overall and a heavy sweater, both too large. She pulled them on, rolled up the sleeves and cuffs. The feel of the rough warm cloth delighted her. She found a pair of football socks and shoved her feet into them, drawing them up like leg warmers. She searched several rooms for a telephone without finding one. Hunger and thirst drove her to the kitchen where she drank several glasses of water and wolfed down three slices of buttered bread. She was careful not to disturb anything. She buttered the bread with the carving knife which, she discovered, she was unwilling to let go.

She ran water in the sink and washed her hands and face, wiping herself dry on the sweater. Oh, Christ, she thought, why isn't there a phone? She began another search and was in one of the front rooms when she heard the car return. A wave of fear and panic swept over her. She couldn't stay in the warmth with the food and the hot water any longer. She ran through the house and out the back door. There was a garden shed seventy metres away, near the wall. She stumbled across the grass and past the covered swimming pool. The shed was unlocked. She went inside and crouched down behind the door, still clutching the knife.

Thornton had driven to the nearest village to buy antiseptic cream, sticking plaster and bandages. The cuts were infecting, he believed, and the arm felt heavy. He'd had much worse in his time and determined to dress the wound thoroughly and forget the discomfort until this episode was ended. He decided to search more systematically than before, although he was confident that the woman couldn't have survived a night in the bush in her condition. He had begun to clean the cuts and apply the cream when he heard a car enter the driveway. He stood by a window with a Beretta Puma automatic in his hand. He was relieved when he saw Ramsay slam the car door and stalk towards the house.

Ramsay was alarmed at Thornton's appearance when they met in the entrance lobby. The retired agent had always been immaculate and in control. Now, wearing only a singlet and trousers and in his stockinged feet, he looked harassed and uncertain. The cuts on his arm were inflamed and the hastily applied cream made them look worse. 'Well?' Ramsay barked.

Thornton shook his head. 'No sign. I just came back to fix this, then I'll go out again. I'm sure she couldn't have got far.'

'Show me what happened. I can scarcely credit your incompetence.'

Thornton completed treating his injury before he escorted Ramsay to the room where Ruth May had been held. Ramsay examined the tracksuit and observed splotches of blood on the floor. Suspicious

179

by nature, he wondered if Thornton was lying to him. Had he perhaps attempted to rape the girl, killed her and instituted this elaborate cover-up? Ramsay pushed the thought away. Not Thornton's style. The woman had simply out-manoeuvred him and then inflicted considerable physical and emotional damage. He could feel Thornton's lack of confidence as he walked through the house. Thornton was turning into a liability when he needed assets. Ramsay tried to remain calm but the thought of Huck, Crawley and Draper converging on the house was enough to panic anybody. Without telling him why, he instructed Thornton to remove all traces of the woman's presence. His mind was running on the possibility of a bluff and the expendability of Thornton.

'Don't miss any of the blood, hers or yours,' Ramsay said sharply.

Thornton took the Beretta from his pocket and pointed it at Ramsay's well-groomed head. 'Enough,' he said.

'What the hell are you doing?'

'I want to know what brought you here. What's going on?'

'You said you weren't interested in the machinations, just the mechanics.'

'That was before, when things were running more or less smoothly. Now they've obviously gone wrong. I take it Draper failed to kill Huck?'

Ramsay looked at the unwavering pistol and nodded.

'It's a relief to know I'm not the only one to make mistakes. Have you made some yourself, Derek? It strikes me suddenly as very odd for you to be here. To expose yourself, as it were. What's the threat?'

Ramsay made his decision. Shaken or not, he needed Thornton. 'Crawley.'

'Then you *have* blundered somehow. All that was your department. Is Crawley coming here?'

'Yes. Huck has apparently got information out of Draper.'

'Huck, too. How much further has this spread?'

Ramsay was surprised at the change in Thornton. He seemed to have grown in stature and confidence during the conversation. He felt his own authority slipping away. 'I don't know,' he muttered. 'The Mainwaring woman knows something, possibly Dacre as well. I'm not sure.'

'That's containable,' Thornton said. 'I know Crawley. He has no subtlety, especially where women are involved. He'll come barging in to play the white knight. Huck is a clod.'

'What are you saying?'

'Derek, you're the head of the Bureau of National Assessment. If you can't make a few arrangements, tidy up a few details, what bloody use are you?'

Ramsay glared at the older man and said nothing, waiting to see what he would propose. Thornton put the pistol down while he struggled into a shirt and a windbreaker. 'Huck and Crawley are bringing Draper out here, you say. I think we can arrange for Draper to kill both of them and not survive himself. Come with me.'

Ramsay followed Thornton into a small room at the back of the house and stared as he opened a cupboard and removed a rifle. Thornton took a telescopic sight and a box of ammunition from a drawer and proceeded to load and sight in the rifle with easy, practised movements. The damage to his arm did not seem to affect him.

'You're enjoying this,' Ramsay said.

'Not exactly. It's rather messy for my taste. I always preferred the operations that went smoothly and where no one was hurt.' He slammed the magazine home and checked the action. 'I won't mind killing Draper, though. I didn't take to him at all.'

'What if Crawley and Huck bring others with them?'

Thornton shook his head. 'They won't. I know them from the garbage collector days in Melbourne. Their behaviour was always so unpleasant and unorthodox that they couldn't stand scrutiny. Crawley has a very high opinion of himself. They'll come alone.'

Ramsay began to feel a little better, almost as if he was regaining his edge. *You're wrong, Gerard*, he thought. *Crawley's changed since the Melbourne days. He's far more subtle than you imagine.* You *might be the blunderer now.*

Thornton handed him the Beretta. 'I'm going up onto the roof. With a bit of luck I'll get all three pretty smartly. You might have to clean up a little. Are you capable of it?'

Ramsay nodded and accepted the pistol. He had no plans to use it but it was a comfort, given that there were several directions in which it could be pointed.

~ 23 ~

Crawley was the first to arrive at the Thistle Creek bridge. He pulled off the road under some water-starved willows and sat on a stump, looking back in the direction he had come for the agents Hector Bain had recruited. After fifteen minutes he accepted the obvious—Hector had lied. Not that it would ever appear that way. There would have been problems with transport, equipment, a failure of communications. Crawley dismissed the reinforcements from his mind and waited for Huck.

When the van arrived he shook hands with Huck and stood back while the back of the van was opened. Toby jumped out, almost bowling Crawley over. He stood his ground and let the dog sniff him. The smell from the van was strong and Crawley wondered what sort of condition Draper was in. Then he saw the New Zealander, looking dishevelled but composed, sitting handcuffed to the wheel housing.

'Gidday, Kiwi. You don't look too bad. Old Hucky must be getting soft.'

'You wouldn't think so if you had my busted fingers and cracked ribs, Crawley. Let's get this over with.'

'Right. Where do we go?'

Draper stared out from the gloom of the van into the pale sunlight. 'I need an independent witness. Otherwise, what guarantees have I got?'

Crawley showed Draper the Browning Hi-Power under his arm. 'Just this. If the girl's all right you'll be able to check into Auckland General casualty tonight. If she's not, you won't have to worry about fingers and ribs.'

'Fifteen minutes away,' Draper said. 'Branch off a kilometre down the road to the right and take a left fork about the same distance further on. Roads are a bit rough. Don't blame me if this crate falls apart.'

'I'll blame you for anything that goes wrong,' Crawley said. 'What's that bloody smell?'

Huck explained as he drove, sucking on the unlit pipe. He told Crawley about Reggie Carmichael and together they reviewed what they knew about Gerard Thornton.

'Hard bastard,' Crawley said. 'But getting a bit long in the tooth, wouldn't you say?'

'Not much older than me,' Huck grunted.

'Right. I'll remember that. He can shoot a bit as I recall. What did you bring?'

They discussed the weaponry. The van bucked and jolted along the rough track. Draper drummed his feet on the floor and Toby, who had reluctantly re-entered the back of the van, barked loudly. Huck stopped the vehicle and pulled off the track. He let Toby out and unfastened the handcuffs. He allowed Draper to swing his arms and stretch before cuffing him again with his hands in front. Draper pointed with his splinted fingers.

'House's through there, behind those trees. High wall, gates in front. Generator, so you can't knock the power out.'

'Who'll be there, apart from Thornton?' Huck asked.

Draper shrugged and winced as the movement hurt him. 'Search me. I've sort of been out of things for a while.'

Crawley checked his pistol. 'Where is she?'

'In a room near the back on the lower level. There's a courtyard behind it where she took the sun.'

'We'll sneak up and take a look front and back. Vehicles, Kiwi?'

'A Merc, that's it.'

The three men advanced through the light scrub beside the road. Huck carried the MP40 on a sling over his shoulder, leaving both hands free. Draper stumbled several times and Toby growled at his heels. The house rose up before them, vast and silent.

'Weird joint,' Huck said. 'Good for the job, I suppose.'

Crawley squinted. 'There's another car out front apart from the Mercedes. Looks like a Rover or something. What d'you know about that?'

Draper shook his head. 'Nothing. Didn't have any bloody callers when I was there.'

'Give me the layout.'

Crawley listened intently as Draper described the configuration of the house. 'Okay. Let's not piss around. Run the van straight in, Hucky, and put the cars out of commission. Then get yourself some cover and see what happens. I'll go over the wall at the back and try to get into the house.'

'Big hero,' Draper sneered.

'Shut up. You'll be in the van with the dog. Your arse is on the line, Kiwi. You better hope everything goes okay.'

'Shit, you're mad. That Rover could've brought in four blokes.'

Crawley shook his head. 'I don't think so. I'm pretty sure that's Derek Ramsay's car. Derek doesn't give rides to the hoi polloi and I'm not too worried about him.'

Huck looked at his watch. 'Ten minutes? Noisy?'

'Make it very noisy,' Crawley said.

Thornton saw the van approach at speed, too fast for him to get a certain shot at the driver. He made allowances for the trajectory and prepared to shoot when the van stopped. *Bull at a gate*, he thought. *You could count on it.* His astonishment at seeing the van skid and its bull-bar slam into the side of Ramsay's Rover distracted him, and before he could shoot, a bulky figure had jumped down, put two bullets into the tyres of the Mercedes and dived for cover back behind the van. Aware of the mistake, but unable to hold back, Thornton fired. The shot threw up gravel from a spot the target had only briefly occupied. Thornton swore, knowing he had given away his position to no good purpose.

He swore again as a burst of automatic fire rattled against the roof close to where he was crouched. He tensed and felt suddenly exposed and vulnerable, with an uncertain purchase on the sloped tiles, and a target with superior fire power. He scuttled awkwardly back towards the attic window and had his good leg over the sill when he heard Huck's voice. He looked down to see Huck standing clear of the van, with the fold-out stock of a machine pistol braced against his shoulder.

'Chuck the rifle down, Gerard. Don't be a mug. I couldn't miss you with this from here.'

Thornton tossed the rifle and heaved himself through the window. Glass, splintered wood and tile fragments followed him but he was unhurt.

Crawley stripped off his suit jacket and threw it up over the strands of barbed wire on top of the wall. He pulled himself up, went gingerly over the covered wire, and braced himself for the long drop into the courtyard. He landed slightly winded, recovered quickly and moved across the bricked surface to a door at the back of the house. He stepped into a passage which led to a short flight of stairs. He went up the stairs quickly, flattened himself against the wall and moved on, following the map of the house clearly etched in his mind from Draper's description.

He found the room where Ruth May had been held, saw the bars, the magazines, the crumpled tracksuit and the splotches of blood. He swore and left the room to see Gerard Thornton coming down a narrow staircase, moving awkwardly on his stiff leg. Crawley brought the Browning up.

'Where is she?' he shouted.

Thornton froze. 'I don't know.'

Crawley's shot tore into the wall and showered Thornton with plaster.

'Where?'

'She got away, Crawley. Escaped. I don't know where she is.'

'Get down here. Keep your hands where I can see them.'

Thornton complied, moving slowly with his hands raised. Crawley gestured for him to continue on towards the front of the house. They went into a wide hallway. Light flooded in above Thornton's head from the stained glass window above the front door.

'I'm going to ask you once more,' Crawley said.

'Crawley, I swear . . .'

Draper stepped through the door with a rifle in his manacled hands. He fired twice into Thornton's back, saw Crawley and threw the rifle down. 'I thought he had you.'

'You murdering bastard. How did you get that gun? Where's Huck?'

'It's Thornton's. Huck got him to throw it down. Then he ducked inside. I told Huck the quickest way up to him but . . .'

'Like hell you did. You sidetracked him and thought you'd play a hand. Well, you outsmarted yourself, Kiwi. Thornton said the girl got away and he couldn't find her. You know where that leaves you.'

'Crawley, I . . .'

Huck appeared from a side passage. 'Shit, Creepy, I'm sorry. Toby saw someone running and went after him. What happened here?'

'Draper's offed Thornton,' Crawley said. 'Thinking to save his hide, but he's wrong. Where's Ramsay?'

Huck was staring at Thornton's body. 'I thought he came in here.'

Ruth May crouched in the darkness of the garden shed. She was disoriented and feverish, had lost track of time and was terrified by scuffling noises around her. She had no particular fear of rats herself, but she remembered Winston Smith's fear of them in *1984* and a passage from the book flashed through her mind:

> *The rat . . . although a rodent, is carnivorous.*
> *You are aware of that. You will have heard of the*
> *things that happen in the poor quarters of this*
> *town. In some streets a woman dare not leave her*
> *baby alone in the house, even for five minutes.*
> *The rats are sure to attack it. Within quite a*
> *small time they will strip it to the bones . . .*

She whimpered and when the crash of cars colliding and the booming sound of the shots reached her she shut her eyes and felt herself slipping towards some kind of madness.

Then she heard a dog barking and the sound of a man running. The door was jerked open and the light momentarily blinded her. A man stood in front of her, gasping. A thick-bodied, older man. Tee, surely, and here she was with it all to do over again. She screamed and lunged forward, plunging the knife into his stomach and ripping upwards and sideways with all her remaining strength. 'I'm not going back into that room,' she screamed. 'Never! Never! Never!'

The dog stopped barking and she saw the man twist away and fall on his back. His hands clutched at the place where blood was spurting and something grey was welling out. She had never seen the man before. He looked surprised and kindly. The world spun. The dog barked again and she fainted. The knife fell and bounced on the grass. The dog nosed at it and howled.

Crawley felt for the pulse in Ramsay's neck. He straightened up and shook his head. 'He's dead.'

Huck quietened Toby and drew away from the body. Draper stood mutely with his cuffed hands clasped in front of him as Crawley examined Ruth May. 'Well?' he said.

'She's fainted. Feels hot. I'd say she's pretty ill.'

'Fuck ill. She's alive, isn't she? All in one piece. What about our deal?'

'Where's the phone?' Crawley said.

Huck was already moving. 'I saw one in the Merc. Who do I call? Hector?'

Crawley nodded. 'Yeah, better keep it all in the family. Get a pillow and a blanket from the house, too.'

'Crawley,' Draper said. 'We had a deal.'

Crawley stood up and put his pistol under Draper's chin. 'It didn't include you killing Thornton. You realise with Ramsay gone we've lost another chance to find out what this was all about. That makes what you know important.'

'I was a hired hand. I don't know a fucking thing.'

'You realise how easy this would be?'

'Yeah. You could do it, but what's the point? I told Huck I didn't kill the woman in Tassie or the bloke on the coast. Thornton did them.'

'Hard to say now, isn't it, one way or the other? What about the halfwit at Coota?'

'An accident. I barely tapped him. And I never laid a hand on this woman. She's a good-looker, too.'

Crawley lowered the pistol and looked down at Ruth. Despite the dishevelment and dirt the resemblance to Mandy was still striking. Her eyelids fluttered. Huck returned with a blanket, a pillow and sheet. He threw the sheet over Ramsay.

'Hector's shitting himself,' Huck said. 'But a team's on the way.'

Crawley arranged Ruth more comfortably. 'You're the last thing she'll want to see, Draper,' he said. 'Uncuff him, Hucky.'

Huck unlocked the handcuffs. Draper cautiously rubbed his wrists and flexed his hands. 'My air ticket's in the house. What's it going to be, Crawley?'

Crawley looked at Huck. 'What d'you reckon?'

Huck shrugged. 'There's enough shit to clear away as it is. I wouldn't mind busting a few more fingers or maybe giving Toby a bite.'

'Luxuries,' Crawley said. 'Take him back to the

house and let him get his stuff. Then you can start walking, Kiwi. If I ever see you again . . .'

'You won't.' Draper turned and walked towards the house. Toby growled. Huck followed with the MP40 at the ready.

Crawley bent and brushed the matted, straggling hair from Ruth May's face. Her lips moved and she muttered something he couldn't catch. 'It's okay,' he said. 'It's all over. Whatever the hell it was.'

~ 24 ~

'I have never,' Hector Bain said, 'had to lift a carpet as high so as to sweep so much dirt under it.'

Crawley had a hangover. He swallowed two aspirins with his coffee. 'Nice command of metaphor, Hector. But you were just doing what you're very good at. Want another medal?'

They were in Bain's office in the early afternoon of the day following the raid on the house at Thistle Creek. The FSA squad had removed the bodies and disabled vehicles, cleaned up the house and repaired the damage. Huck had returned to the coast. Ruth May was installed in Crawley's house, recuperating. Mandy was expected back from Melbourne that evening. Crawley was looking forward to seeing the meeting of the cousins, but nothing else pleased him. With Rupert Dacre in the United States and Ramsay and Thornton dead, there seemed no way to discover what the operation had been about, what the deaths were for. Bain sipped his coffee, enjoying the sight of Crawley frustrated.

'What the hell are you looking happy about, Hector? We're still completely in the dark with this thing. I guess you're safe in your seat again. Is that all you ever worry about?'

'By no means. And I doubt that my position was ever unsafe. You made your attitude to the job perfectly clear, and do you really imagine that Derek Ramsay would have contrived to replace me with Dacre?'

'Maybe not. But it goes against the grain not to know what was in their bloody minds.'

'How much would you give to know?'

'What d'you mean?'

'Exactly what I say. What do you think it would be worth to have a clear account of the motives and objectives of Ramsay, Dacre and Thornton?'

Crawley's head throbbed as he tried to engage with the question. Although Bain had taken the credit for the clean-up of the mess, Crawley had put in a lot of time on it himself. And he had visited Boris Stein in hospital as well as seeing to the care and comfort of Ruth May, who had refused to go anywhere but to Crawley's house. Then he had talked late into the night with Huck. They discussed retirement, talked about becoming security consultants, or private inquiry agents, reviewed old friends and enemies. Crawley drank a lot, Huck very little before he left in the battered van after two hours' sleep on the Crawley sofa.

'It'd be good to know,' Crawley grunted. 'Whatever it was, Ramsay and Thornton weren't up to it. Too old. But there's no way . . .'

'What if we had had an agent in place from the start? Close to the conspirators?'

'Bullshit.'

Bain took a sheet of paper from the desk and slid it across towards Crawley who made a grab for it. He groaned and held his head. 'Don't make me make sudden movements. What's this?'

'Read it.'

Crawley ran his eyes over the sheet. It confirmed a promotion for Mrs Carol Mainwaring to two grades above her present rank and endorsed her application to make a study tour to Europe and the United States for three months on full pay and with a generous *per diem* allowance. The document required the signature of the director and another senior FSA officer. Crawley felt the throbbing in his head recede. 'She wrote this, didn't she?'

Bain nodded. 'More or less. A bit of give and take. We've spent a good part of the morning negotiating.'

'She claims to know all about it?'

'Absolutely everything, so she says.'

'Any proof offered?'

Bain shrugged. 'Not really. She claims to have a tape of a statement made by Dacre. She says she talked to him in the National Gallery restaurant shortly after our meeting and that he explained everything to her. He, of course, was innocent of any direct involvement in the . . . nastiness. She says the same of herself. I have independent confirmation that such a meeting took place—you'll remember that we had someone watching her—but nothing more.'

Crawley tapped the paper. 'We sign this and she tells all?'

'She's waiting outside.'

Crawley signed the letter with a flourish and slid it back across the desk to Bain who did the same. He pressed a button on his console and said, 'Show Mrs Mainwaring in, please.'

Carol Mainwaring looked like a photographic fashion model come to life. Her lilac linen suit fitted her precisely and the black silk blouse matched the severity of her hairstyle. She strutted on very high heels, carrying herself perfectly upright. She scarcely glanced at Crawley and concentrated on Hector Bain as she came to a stop in front of the desk. 'Well?'

Bain passed the signed paper to her. She read it and dropped it back on the polished surface. She stepped sideways, sat in one of Bain's commodious chairs, opened her shoulder bag and took out a gold cigarette case.

Crawley laughed. 'Don't overplay it, Carol.'

She extracted and lit a cigarette. 'You're going to feel very foolish.'

'Who are you talking to?' Bain asked.

'Both of you. I have the tape here. Do you want me to play it or tell it in my own words?'

'Let's hear you first,' Crawley said. 'Tapes are only tapes. A live performance is the real thing.'

Carol butted the cigarette in the pristine ashtray. She relaxed back into the chair and looked at a point somewhere above Bain's head. 'The chief concern was to get a sixty-year protection for early FSA and BNA records.'

'We know that,' Bain said.

Carol smiled. 'But do you know why?'

Bain was determined not to be outdone in urbanity. He locked his hands behind his head and stared at the ceiling. 'It's bloody obvious—because those files contain highly sensitive and dangerous material. Let us speculate—dangerous to certain interests and individuals who are still . . . players, in politics, intelligence, industry . . .'

'No. Completely reasonable, but completely wrong. That's what everyone was meant to think.'

Crawley could taste the sourness of his breath. He had a feeling that he knew what was coming and, despite his ambivalence about his twenty-year plus career in the FSA, he didn't know that he wanted to hear it.

Bain moved the sullied ashtray out of his line of vision. 'Go on.'

'Throughout the whole period from the formation

of the FSA and the BNA right up until the computerisation of the records, for every real operation the
services mounted three or four sham ones were put into
the files.'

Bain's jaw dropped. 'Sham?'

'False, phoney, cooked-up, faked, whatever you like
to call it. Some were purely paper fantasies, others had
some basis in fact but nothing real ever happened,
others were aborted almost at once but the illusion was
created that they continued on.'

'I don't believe it,' Bain said.

Crawley scratched his bristled chin. Today he had
reverted to his usual casual costume and the morning's
shave had been none too close on account of his shaking
hand. 'I do. I was there. It's entirely possible. In those
days there was always a lot of activity that never
seemed to have to do with anything. It was all rigidly
stratified and each level knew bugger all about what
the others did.'

'You're saying that Sir Malcolm French and Toby
Campion . . .'

'Toby Campion didn't have a truthful bone in his
body. He would have loved it.'

Bain stared at Carol Mainwaring, who was looking
at Crawley. Her thin lips were slightly parted and she
had lost her domineering manner. 'What was the
purpose?'

Carol reached out and took the letter. 'Funds,
manpower, perks, prestige. According to Dr Dacre it
was all quite easily managed with the connivance of
certain highly placed people—administrators, agents
and archivists. But computerisation brought it to an
end. CD Roms can be instantly cross-referenced. You
just can't hide things.'

'Is that all?' Bain said.

'No.'

'My god, what?'

'When the records were put on CD Roms some of the false material was excised, but not much. It's mostly still there, scarcely protected by easy-to-crack codes. If a lot of FOI enquiries are directed to it and as it becomes available under the thirty-year rule, the falsification will become apparent.'

Bain groaned.

Carol went on inexorably. 'Hence the need for the longer protection and the exemption from FOI. They were trying to buy time to find a solution.'

'By faking blackmailers, dangerous leaks, by creating an atmosphere of threat,' Crawley said. 'By killing people and kidnapping.'

'I don't know anything about that,' Carol said hastily.

'I take it the terms of that letter are the price of your silence, Mrs Mainwaring?' Bain said.

Carol nodded.

Bain's hand shot out. 'The tape?'

Carol took an audio cassette from her bag and put it on the desk. 'I have a copy.'

'Of course. I think that will be all.'

Crawley watched her close her bag, stand and stride from the room. The sexual attraction was still there and he fancied it was mutual. He didn't blame her for finding a way to save her hide. He thought she would be interesting to work with in the future, if he had a future in this business. He needed to talk to Mandy.

'Well, Ray,' Bain said. 'What do you think?'

'It's a question of whether to come clean or stay dirty.'

'Yes, exactly. And what's your view?'

Crawley stood. 'Up to you. Like I told you, Hector, I wouldn't want your job for twice the pay and half the work.'

'Ah . . . it's early days, but what if I were to make a move to the BNA? I understand the minister's well disposed.'

'Are you offering me your comfortable chair, Hector? What about the car and the expense sheet?'

'We're talking hypothetically, but certainly, yes, why not?'

'You're amazing. You're going to cover it up, aren't you?'

'It must be considered as an option. I imagine it will be a computer matter to a great extent. How is Mr Stein doing?'

'He'll be all right.'

'Good. Good. Teamwork is . . . Where are you going?'

Crawley sauntered towards the door, slapping the pockets of his leather jacket for his car keys. 'I don't know, Hector. I thought I might go and try and find a couple of journalists to talk to. Or a publisher. It might be time to write my memoirs.'

Bain watched the door close. Then he lowered his head towards the desk.

Crawley opened the door again. 'Only kidding,' he said.

Browning P.I.

The big black car came up out of nowhere ... I heard a siren and slowed down and pulled over like an honest citizen. The next thing I knew two men with hats pulled down over their eyes and sunglasses on above their tough expressions were pulling open the front doors of my car. I heard May Lin Scream and I saw a gun ...

Hollywood. Studio screenwriter Hart Sallust, well-known patron of sleazy bars and nightclubs, has disappeared. Peter McVey, private eye, has been hired to find him. In unfamiliar territory, McVey enlists Browning — part-time actor, part-time private eye — at home in any Hollywood bar.

From Hollywood bars to the Chinese underworld, their search uncovers the beautiful May Lin. With Sallust when he disappeared, and seemingly inconsolable. Or is she? Her story has 'more holes in it than a flyscreen'.

This fast-paced, witty novel from Peter Corris features a cameo appearance from Raymond Chandler — master crime-writer and friend of McVey's. His advice: find out what Sallust was writing when he disappeared ...

Browning Battles On

One of the bayonets came to rest just below my Adam's apple. I looked down at the shiny steel and then slowly looked along the length of the rifle barrel up into the face of my executioner. He wore thick glasses with metal rims and he had gold fillings in his teeth. I could see the teeth because he was smiling.

All Richard Browning expects is to go through the motions of making a propaganda film, wear an officer's uniform, stay in a few fancy hotels and enjoy the fleshpots of war-time Sydney. Instead, he is force to slog through the Queensland jungle, dodge bullets and bombs and endure the discomforts of a military prison.

As Browning ducks and weaves in and out of trouble, his companions in strife are 'Harry' Kaminaga, Hawaiian-born Japanese soldier, and Ushi Tanvier, Darlinghurst prostitute. His friendship with the hell-raising actor, Peter Finch, offers him some prospect of escape from his problems, but his enemies in Military Intelligence and among the blackmarket racketeers of the big smoke don't see why he should survive World War II.

Coming home wasn't meant to be like this ...

The Azanian Action

'Ms Clair Mbotho. What do you know about her?'
'I don't know anything about Ms Mbotho. Suppose you tell me all about her ...'
Bain nodded. 'Smarter than the average Bantu. Smarter than the average anyone.'
'I like her already,' Crawley said.
'That's good, because you're going to have to look after her while we untangle several messes she's got herself and us into ...'

Mandela is free, things are changing and South African nationalists Clair Mbotho and Wesley Keta have come to Australia. Ray Crawley's job is to protect Clair; but other forces are at work, and Clair's brutal murder is something Crawley takes very personally.

As the trail leads from Canberra to Sydney to the south coast, Crawley and Huck are drawn into a deadly labyrinth of deception within the intelligence community, racial politics and revenge.

The Japanese Job

Crawley liked the Brisbane of the 90s. The new buildings, the feeling that he could walk down whichever side of the pavement he wanted to. He like the post-Fitzgerald changes for the most part too — new, leaner faces in government and the police. But there were worrying signs of the Yakuza moving in and of the rear-guard action by the white shoe brigade. And who were the Diggers? And how did a leading Japanese businessman end up encased in cement with a length of reinforcing rod through his heart?

Crawley and Huck are drawn into a conflict between the ruthless Japanese corporate world and shadowy Australian interest.

Throats are cut and bodies are buried as Crawley and Huck try to stay on top of *The Japanese Job* …